LUNA

BOOK ONE

THE COVENANT OF SHADOWS

CARA CLARE

For all the thirty-something women who spent the last ten years being wife material and are now absolutely feral.

You fucking deserve some happiness.

Claim your joy, live your life, and buy a Womanizer™ Best self-care on the planet.

For a comprehensive list of content warnings, please visit: www.caraclare.com

THE QUEEN OF SHADOWS

In the depths of night, when shadows grow long,
A child of light emerges, both fragile and strong.
Born of human flesh, yet touched by the dark,
Her soul is a canvas for shadows to mark.

The Queen of Shadows, hidden in plain sight,
Unaware of the power that stirs in the night.
Her blood sings with magic of ages untold,
A force that the ancients once sought to control.

The Covenant of Shadows, a scroll of old,
Holds secrets and powers, both wicked and bold.
It binds the darkness, commands the dead,
An army of shadows, by her to be led.

When she finally rises to the truth of her role,
The world shall tremble, both fragile and whole.

CARA CLARE

For in her *hands lies the fate of all,*
The power to raise or to let kingdoms fall.

PROLOGUE

When your asshole boyfriend walks out on you in the middle of the night to start a new life, the last thing you expect is to receive a delivery of his cock in a box two months later.

But that's exactly what I was faced with.

A cock in a box.

At work.

And let me tell you, it wasn't *that* attractive when it was alive. Dead, it was frankly disgusting.

But I'm getting ahead of myself.

Let's circle back to the evening of the delivery...

CHAPTER 1
LUNA

The alley in front of the bookshop where I work is giving off its usual spooky but quaint vibes. It's dark outside – because it's Cambridge, and the middle of winter, and England is dark pretty much all day at this time of year.

There's a strange kind of mist in the air that's been hanging around the city lately. Creeping in after sunset in a way that reminds me of marshes on the coast instead of the winding streets of a big city.

I open the door and breathe in the crisp evening air. When it's cold out, the shop is either freezing or too hot. All we have are old electric heaters to warm the space – despite the fact I've told my boss via email at least one hundred times that the fluctuating temperature isn't good for the books.

Above me, the shop's glossy black sign swings gently in the breeze. It creaks as it moves, which reminds me of the way my body feels.

Achy.

Protesting under the pressure of even the slightest touch.

This line of thought leads me to the kind of conscious awareness of my pain levels that I try to avoid. Because thinking about pain is even more tiresome than talking about pain.

It starts with noticing that my forearms are sore, then my lower back, my hips, the strange throbbing feeling that seems to embed itself deep in my muscles. All of them. Like I'm recovering from a marathon I never ran.

Rubbing the small of my back, I nudge my glasses further up my nose, then lean against the doorframe and watch as a woman in a beige overcoat and bright red shoes trots down the alleyway toward the market square.

Her heels aren't too tall, but they are tall enough to make me jealous.

I haven't worn heels since before the accident.

I pretend I don't mind – that I'm okay with perpetually being the shortest person in the room – but really, it's hard to feel anything but dowdy when I have to go out wearing flats or trainers.

Steven always told me heels were for *other* women. Not me. That he couldn't imagine a version of me who wore pointy shoes and danced all night, and he was glad he never met *that* Luna.

Of course, he was glad; *that* Luna would never have fallen for his charms. She would never have been so in need of affection and affirmation that she allowed herself to tumble head-first into his web.

Or maybe she would.

Maybe I romanticize that version of myself; the girl who danced all night, snuck out to parties, and felt *alive*.

Since Steven disappeared, even though it's only been two months, I've seen glimmers of *that* Luna. But whenever she tries to claw her way to the surface, it seems like the pain swallows her up, bites down on her, keeps her silent and still and scared.

I have a burst of energy.

A bubbling, irrepressible need to move, to flail my limbs, to scream, and shout, and wear big earrings, and bright colors, and *high heels*.

It lasts a millisecond.

And then his voice creeps in. The fear that he might not really be gone. The sense that he might be lurking just around the corner, watching me. Waiting for me to act out so he can punish me for it.

A shiver runs through me.

I'm ducking back inside, ready to close up for the night, when I hear wheels and the chug of a moped engine. When I turn around, the delivery driver is waving at me. "Delivery for The Haunted Bookshop," he says loudly.

Yes, I work at a shop called *The Haunted Bookshop*. No, it's not really haunted. At least, I've never seen any evidence of ghosts.

I sigh and pinch the bridge of my nose as the delivery driver lifts up his visor. My boss has a habit of sending me books he's purchased at auction on an almost weekly basis. Always old, beautiful editions that – while wonderful to look at – will never sell.

I've asked him to slow down, or move us to a bigger shop, but he has so far ignored both requests.

I linger in the doorway. The driver opens the holdall on the back of the moped.

He makes me sign a small tablet with my index finger, then hands me a large box. I wince, anticipating its weight. But it's definitely lighter than the usual packages we receive; perhaps the books inside are paperbacks – or those strange old penny dreadful pamphlets that the boss seems to be obsessed with.

The driver is gone before I can confirm who the package is from.

Usually, as soon as the shops either side of me close and the alley grows quiet, I lock the door. Since Steven disappeared, especially, it has felt prudent to make sure no one can just walk in when my back's turned.

But tonight, because of the box, I forget.

I leave it unlocked, and the sign turned to *open*, then put the box on the counter and find a knife to slice through the tape on top.

Moving aside the packing, my fingers meet something smooth and hard. I peer inside. A glimpse of dark, coffee-colored wood makes me reach in with both hands.

Using my elbows to knock the cardboard box to the floor, I pull out a smaller wooden one. Glossy wood. Ornate carvings.

I set it down on top of a stack of paperwork.

Something flutters inside me but I'm not sure if it's dread or anticipation and, I swear, the lights flicker as I run my hands over the lid.

It is both smooth and sharp at the same time. There is no lock, but there is a latch. I flip it open and hesitate, fingers on the lip of the lid.

I brush the carvings on top — vines, roses, a moon, and two crucifixes. I can feel my pulse beating in my fingertips, pressing down on the wood, thudding as if the box has a rhythm of its own.

My breath catches in my chest.

My heart is racing.

It is as if the entire world has slowed down, as if something inside this box is calling to a deep, dark part of myself I didn't know existed.

My entire body feels alive. The pain is still there, but it's like a whisper. A memory of pain that I can't latch onto because something else is taking its place.

The lights flicker again.

I lift the lid.

It creaks like the sign outside.

At first, there is darkness. Shadows swell in my vision. I pull the box a little closer, and it makes a strange sound against the papers on the desk. I lift it up. There is a deep red stain grazing the top sheet of paper.

Like scarlet mixed with crimson.

Instead of looking into the box, I look under it. I run my finger along the bottom edge then stare at it.

Deep, velvety redness coats my pale skin. Like I've cut myself, except I haven't. It's not my blood.

The scent tingles in my nose.

I have always been sensitive to the smell of blood; but I have never been squeamish. In fact – and I know this sounds weird – I've always been kind of drawn to it.

As a child, if I grazed my knee or scraped my elbow, I would press my finger to the wound then, when no one was looking, I'd taste the blood. The tang on my tongue would make me feel alive.

I would let it rest there, aware this was not something normal girls did, but enjoying it all the same.

This blood, however, tastes sour. It makes me wrinkle my nose and wipe my hand on my jeans.

The blood continues to drip. Faster now. Some of it falls onto the large, beautiful volume of *Unleash The Magick Within* that I'd been saving up for. It soaks almost instantly into the pale blue cloth cover.

I still haven't looked into the box.

I should feel afraid, shouldn't I?

A normal person, if they received a package containing a box dripping with blood, would panic. Drop it. Scream and run into the street flailing their arms about.

But I am delaying looking, not because I'm afraid, but because I don't want the anticipation to be over.

The lights flicker again.

My vision darkens at its edges, turning the room into a vignette of itself, with shadows closing in.

I'm shaking now.

Because whatever is inside this box is going to change my life.

I can't explain how I know. I just do.

Finally, I set the box back down, take a deep breath, and peer inside.

The first thing I notice is a soft velvet cushion, which looks like it used to be purple but is now almost black from the blood it has absorbed.

The second thing I notice is what's sitting on top of the cushion; a tangled, bloodied mass of...

Body parts?

The sort of things you find in the back room of a butcher's shop.

Except... human? Human body parts.

I reach in and nudge them.

Told you, not squeamish.

Beneath them, drenched in blood, is a note. I tug it free and try to decipher the blood-soaked handwriting.

Luna,

He cannot hurt you anymore.

Every part of him that ever disrespected you has been removed from his worthless body.

You no longer need to be afraid.

I will always protect you.

It is then, right then, in that moment, as I read the word *disrespected,* that I realize what they are.

A hand.

A tongue.

An eye.

And...

Oh shit. I know what *that* is. And, sure, it could belong to anyone. I mean, one penis is pretty much like the next, right? But I know – just *know* – it is Steven's.

They are all his.

Pieces of him.

His hand. Pinching my arm. *Listen to me Luna. Are you listening?*

His eye. Steely. Pale blue. Assessing my body with disdain. With hate. Not love.

His tongue. *You fat, frigid, pathetic whore.*

His cock. *You never want it. What's wrong with you?*

Bile and vomit rise in my stomach, but then turn to something else.

I reach inside and lift out the hand. I rub at the spot just below the thumb until... there it is. A mole that looks like the number six. I used to wonder why there weren't two more of them.

666.

The devil's numbers.

I drop it back in and place my hands firmly on either side of the box. They are covered in blood and leave dark handprints on the desk.

Laughter fizzes and crackles in my lungs.

He would never have imagined this could happen to him. He would never even have dreamed someone could have this kind of power over him.

But someone has.

Someone took him apart, piece by piece, and they did it for me.

I will always protect you.

All that fear and worry that he was right around the corner about to jump out at me. And the entire time, he's been in bits.

Dismantled.

The way he dismantled me for so many years.

Next, I lift out Steven's tongue. Because of all the things he ever did to me, the things he said, the words he carved in the deepest crevices of my psyche, and which grew deeper, and heavier, turning my soul to blackness – those were the worst.

Looking at it in my palm, I almost expect the tongue to have a pulse. To start lapping at my skin, trying to find its way back to the Steven-shaped body that lies dismembered somewhere in the dark.

I drop the tongue and it lands with a sound that makes me start to shake.

I grip the edge of the counter and try to breathe.

This time, the laughter does turn to vomit. I puke onto the floor. Some of it splashes my shoes.

Who, and how, and why, and when circle in my head, pound against the inside of my skull.

Whatever glimmer of strength and power I felt when I realized Steven was gone has instantaneously morphed into something else.

Fear.

Solidifying like ice in my veins.

What do I do with them?

Do I tell the police?

Everyone thinks Steven left me for the woman he'd been having an affair with. The detectives showed me transcripts of their online chats, texts, his search history, proof that his car had driven up to Scotland then disappeared somewhere in the Highlands.

But he can't have.

Because he is here. In pieces. In my hands.

The eye.

The hand.

They are unmistakably his.

And now they are mine.

But what the fuck do I do with them?

CHAPTER 2
LUNA

I am still staring at the tongue on the floor when the bell above the door jingles and a rush of cold air sweeps into the room. The papers on the desk flutter. But only a little. They are weighed down by the box and the blood.

I look up in a panic and reach for the box.

But the person in the doorway isn't moving. They are stock still, wearing a large grey hoodie, a black leather jacket, and torn jeans. I look at their feet. They are bare. Red toenails.

Bare feet?

Bare feet.

Shit. It's freezing outside, so the only reason someone would be wandering around with no shoes on is if they can't feel the cold.

And there's only one type of creature who can't feel the extremes of hot and cold the way humans do.

I move quickly to the other side of the desk, shielding the box from view.

I'm staring at a vampire. I have a box full of bloody body parts in my shop, and a tongue lying on the floor, and a vampire is standing in the doorway.

"I'm sorry, we're about to close."

I should have locked the goddamn door.

"I'm not here for the books," says a raspy female voice that sounds like it should smell of cigarettes.

The box. It's the fucking box. The smell of the blood brought her here.

She is breathing heavily. I can see her chest rising and falling. She tilts her head. The motion is jerky and not quite natural. I try to look into the shadows of her face and catch sight of her features, but there is nothing there.

Until... a flash of red.

She pushes her hood away from her face.

Her eyes are sparkling with small red dots.

Again, the lights overhead flicker, and I feel like the ice in my veins is melting, slowing down, turning to sludge.

I try to move but my feet are planted flat on the floor and my legs are not cooperating.

Shadows shift and swell in the corners of my vision as if I'm dangerously close to passing out.

The way they did in the accident.

Fear crawls down my limbs. Sharp fingernails of dread, clawing the underside of my skin and making the hairs on the back of my neck stand on end.

She is a vampire.

The way she moves, the red freckles in her eyes. She looks like an apex predator assessing her prey.

When she does open her mouth, I know for sure. Her bright white fangs catch the light. At first, I'm transfixed. But then my fascination morphs back into fear.

I look at the door. I'll never make it.

I look back at the vampire.

I have never seen one like her before. Despite all the talk and the whispers. Despite them being out in the open in so many other parts of the world. Here, in Cambridge, we like to pretend we don't have the *bad* kind of supers; only the ones who hold respectable jobs and integrate nicely into human society.

Even then, their *different* nature is barely acknowledged or talked about.

We have been taught to recognize them, but we like to believe our vampires are more civilized than all the others.

Except they're not; they're just sneakier.

And this vampire – the one standing in front of me right now – she is not the civilized kind. She has blood lust in her eyes.

By her sides, her fingers twitch. They are splayed wide as if she is preparing for a fight.

"What's in the box, little girl?" she asks, taking a long, deep breath and licking her lips.

The box. Of course, she's here because of the box.

I should give it to her. Hand it over. Let her devour the parts of Steven I never want to see again. But something inside me feels indignant. They were a gift. To me. I finally own a piece of him, and I don't want to let it go. Not so soon.

Even though a vampire eating what's left of him would solve the issue of whether or not to tell the police.

She takes a step forward. Then the door jingles again. Another figure appears, and another, then a fourth.

They stand in line, predators waiting to circle their prey.

I reach for the box and toss it to the floor in front of them. I might want to own Steven, but I want to keep living, too. I'm not going to sacrifice myself for the want of feeling as if I've got one over on him.

The first vamp looks down at the box, then lets out a long dry laugh. "You think that's what we want?"

"Isn't it?" My voice comes out thready and frail, like it might crack completely and turn to dust.

"Not now we've seen what else is on offer." The one nearest the door speaks. He is wearing sweatpants and a t-shirt, not even close to enough clothing for how cold it is outside, and now draws closer to me.

My eyes move around the room. I have nothing to protect myself with. No crucifixes, or silver, or stakes, or garlic.

Not that garlic is a real thing. It's a myth.

Perhaps the rest are, too.

"I'm not sure I'm as tasty as you think." I tip my chin up and try to speak over the vicious pounding of my heart against my ribs. "I take pain meds. My blood will be bitter." I wrinkle my nose. "I'm sure you've had far better."

The man, who is now only a few feet away from me, blinks a few times then claps his hands. "Poor, sweet, human," he says. "You just made yourself an even tastier treat. Skin like yours... so fragile, so ready to be broken. *And* drug-laced blood. What could be better?" He looks back at the vampires behind him. The one in the hoodie strides forward and elbows him out of the way.

She is on me before I even realize what is happening.

She has my arm. Her fingers tighten like a vice around my wrist.

"If every human in this city is as naive as you," she says, "we are going to have our fill now the queen is gone and we've got a *real* boss in charge. One who understands the value of asserting our dominance on the pathetic, weak, blood-sacks of this city."

"Queen?" I murmur.

She grins at me, licking her fangs. "Would you like me to start here..." She presses a finger to my wrist. "Or here?" She trails it up my arm to my neck, to where my pulse is growing faster by the second.

I cannot speak.

I cannot move.

The lights flicker. The shadows groan. I'm going to pass out. I'm going to feint and she's going to devour me, and I'll never find out what really happened to Steven. I'll never have truly mind-blowing sex, or swim naked in the river under the moon and stars, or—

She brings my wrist to her lips and bites down. Hard. Pain ricochets down my arm, sweeping every other sensation from my body.

I cannot fight her.

I'm going to die.

The other vamps are closing in, like those vicious grey dinosaurs from *Jurassic Park* who hunt in packs, when the door clatters back on its hinges.

The sound swallows the tingle of the bell. The entire building seems to shake.

The vampire holding me spins around, pulling me against her so my back is pressed to her chest, and wraps one arm tight around my neck.

She hisses, baring her fangs, staring at the door.

There is a blur of movement.

In a fraction of a second, she is on the floor, neck snapped, blank eyes staring up at the ceiling.

The other three vampires try to run, but the blur of movement engulfs them too.

The first one, the male who taunted me, doesn't even have time to scream before his head is wrenched from his body. It falls to the ground with a sickening thud, his lifeless eyes still wide with shock.

The two remaining vampires turn to face their attacker. They bare their fangs, hissing and snarling like cornered animals. But there is no one there.

Until...

I stagger backward. I tread on Steven's tongue. The feel of it beneath the sole of my shoe makes me jerk sideways, heart pounding.

In the center of the room, a vampire I've seen twice before flexes his fingers and bares his fangs.

Thornfield.

Professor Lucien Thornfield.

When did he come to the shop? A couple of months ago?

Once when I was with Steven, then again looking for some obscure text on shifters.

Bear shifters.

Was he this good looking then?

Tilting his head from side to side, he shrugs off his dark brown suit jacket to reveal muscular shoulders encased in a crisp white shirt. He's wearing braces, black with silver buckles, and runs his thumb under one of them as he assesses the two remaining vampires.

If he *was* this hot before, I didn't notice. I mean, I noticed he was kind of smolder-y. But not turn-a-girl-on-when-she's-fighting-for-her-life levels of smolder.

It's the shoulders.

And the braces.

Fuck, Luna. Get a grip.

"Thornfield..." One of the vamps mutters. She glances at the other.

Thornfield holds up a hand to silence them, then turns to me. "Luna, are you all right?"

I nod at him. The sound of my name on his lips makes my mouth go dry.

"You're quite sure?"

I nod again.

He narrows his eyes, clocks the blood on my hands, the box on the counter, the tongue on the floor. Then turns back to my assailants.

"Did you hear about what happened to the queen?" Thornfield growls, inching closer to them.

The vamps furtively look at the door as if they're assessing whether they can make it out before he catches them.

Deciding they can't, the female says, "We heard."

"Tell me." He rolls up his sleeves, reaches into his pocket, and takes out a cigar.

Panic blooms in my stomach.

He lights it and draws it to his lips.

I clear my throat.

Thornfield turns his gaze on me and quirks an eyebrow. Amusement and irritation dart across his face.

"The books," I hiss, gesturing to the cigar. "The smoke..."

There is a pause. Then, slowly, Thornfield uses the palm of his hand to put out the cigar. It sizzles as it meets his flesh, but when he drops it to the floor and uncurls his fingers, his skin is already sewing itself back together.

"You were saying?" he asks the quivering vampires.

"You killed her," says one.

"Ate her heart," mutters the other.

I wrap my arms around my waist. He *ate* someone's heart?

"Why did I do that?" Thornfield folds his arms. His muscles twitch.

"To prove you're the boss," the muttering one says.

"To prove I'm the boss." Thornfield starts to smile. "Exactly."

"Except..." The female tries to answer him. There's a flash of defiance in her eyes. But then there is another blur of movement and a stomach-churning *crack*.

I slam my eyes closed.

When I open them, both of the remaining vampires lie on the floor. The sides of their skulls are caved in. Did he smash their heads together?

Thornfield towers over them, then crouches down.

They are still alive, their eyes twitching strangely in their concave faces.

He taps one on the forehead then takes hold of their chin and makes them look at me. "Apologize to the lady," he says.

A slurred, unintelligible sound chokes past their lips.

With just a click of his fingers, he makes the other vampire do the same.

Then he stands, takes a handkerchief from his pocket, and uses it to wipe his hands.

"You are quite sure you're alright?" he asks, his voice dripping down my skin like smooth, shining obsidian.

I nod mutely, my heart still racing. I glance at the bodies littering the floor.

Thornfield steps closer, his movements cautious now, as if trying not to startle me further.

One of the vamps on the floor moans and starts dragging their limp carcass toward the door. They are inches away from Thornfield. He steps on their hand. They moan again, and the crunching sound makes me wince.

"We need to go." Thornfield fixes his gaze on mine. "There may be more of them coming."

He extends a hand toward me. I hesitate for a moment, my mind reeling.

"Why would there be more?"

He places a large, strangely warm hand on my forearm. He narrows his eyes at me. "Lately, there are always more."

Once again, Thornfield offers me his hand.

"We will discuss this more when we are somewhere safe."

"Safe?"

Thornfield trails his fingers up my arms, leaving sparks of heat in their wake.

"I will always protect you, Luna."

My eyes dart to the wooden box on the counter as realization washes over me.

"You killed Steven..."

He hesitates for a fraction of a second then nods almost imperceptibly. "I taught him a lesson."

"You mailed him to me in a box!"

"Not all of him."

I pull back, step away, putting space between us. I haven't thought about my pain since the box arrived. But suddenly, my limbs start to ache.

I rub my forearms.

I look at the box, then the door.

Thornfield tilts his head as if he's heard something, and when he turns back to me his eyes are dark inky pools, swimming with urgency.

"We have to go now, Luna."

I stare at him, shaking.

I have a choice. Refuse to go with him, and wait for more vampires to descend, or take his hand.

Wait for death?

Or trust a guy who tore my ex-boyfriend apart to *protect* me?

I'm still trying to decide when Lucien Thornfield grabs me by the waist and tosses me over his shoulder. "I said, time to go," he growls.

CHAPTER 3
LUCIEN

TWO MONTHS AGO

When I reach the bookshop, I pause and tilt my face up to the air. I inhale deeply. There she is...

It is seven p.m. Her shift ended an hour ago, and yet I still sense her on the breeze.

I follow her scent.

Through side streets, across the green. Until I come to a small, terraced house. The kind that looks unassuming but costs a small fortune to rent.

I should know; I own ten of them.

Not this one, though.

This one is different. It has been modernized – new windows, new door, incongruously neat paving in the small front garden.

The lights are on. A dull orange glow comes from the living room.

I approach in the shadows and peer in. Here, I don't just smell her – I smell *him* too.

The boyfriend.

From the very first time he picked her up from the shop after work, I had my suspicions about him. He is the kind of man who thinks too much of himself too often. Who moves through the world as if he expects everyone to bask in his brilliance, and who wants nothing more than to capture Luna's light and twist it for his own pleasure.

If he was a kind, honorable man who treated her the way she deserves to be treated, I'd be able to sit back and enjoy watching them together. Knowing she was taken care of.

But him? I could never enjoy watching her with him.

The thought of *him* fills me with pure, unadulterated rage.

When she comes into view, I lick my fangs and heat pools at the base of my spine.

I have been watching her for years.

Usually, I see her dressed for work. But now, I'm staring at her in nothing but a towel. Pristine and white, it is wrapped tightly around her, but strains across her breasts and her hips.

Her hair is wrapped in a towel too, but when she sits down on the couch opposite the fireplace, she removes it and shakes her curls free. Wet, they look much darker than they are. But they hang in delicious ringlets around her face.

A bead of water escapes from the tip of one of the curls and trickles down between her breasts.

Hell damn it, I want to lick that water from her skin.

I didn't always feel this way about her. When I first started watching her, it was a favor. The Human Extinction League were looking for someone. They thought she might be the one they needed. I thought it would be useful to have them indebted to me. So, I agreed.

They probably thought I'd assign it to one of my men.

But the second I saw Luna, I knew she was mine to watch.

Mine to protect.

Now, holding the towel in her hands, she twists it, her knuckles pale with the pressure. Then she leans forward. Her shoulders begin to shake.

Just like that... she is crying.

My stomach constricts with something I am not used to feeling.

I have never seen her cry before.

There is movement further back in the room. It's *him*.

Steven emerges holding two glasses of red wine. He hands her one. She looks at it and wipes the tears from her cheek with the back of her hand. I can tell from the expression on her face that she does not like the wine, but he stands over her and watches until she drinks.

She takes a sip.

He keeps staring.

She takes another.

When she tries to put it down, he tweaks his finger beneath it and makes her keep drinking. He pushes harder. She can't drink fast enough. The wine spills down her chin and drips onto the towel. She coughs.

He stops.

He takes the glass away and puts it down with a thud on the table. Then he points to the stain on the towel she's wearing. His face darkens.

She is shaking.

He stoops down, stares at her, his face barely a breath away from hers. "You fat, miserable, frigid, whore," he spits.

She swallows hard, almost choking on her tears.

He takes hold of her upper arm and squeezes tight, pinching

her soft flesh with his large fingers. She winces, but he doesn't let go. Instead, he uses the other hand to unfasten his belt.

Rage swells inside me. It beats a savage rhythm in the crevices of my ribcage, straining, cracking, exploding.

Oh, fuck, no.

I might be able to bite down on the urge to rip him apart when he's talking down to her and belittling her. But this?

Fuck. No.

I move to the front door and rap hard with a clenched fist.

It takes every ounce of willpower I possess not to jerk it open and tear him apart in front of her.

But I'm smarter than that.

I hear him mumble for her to stay where she is. Not to move.

He pulls open the door. His eyes widen. But my hand is around his throat before he can utter a single word.

I should have done this a long time ago.

As I drag him into the shadows, I whisper, "You're about to learn an important lesson, Steven. Are you ready?"

"You're the guy who came into Luna's shop. The professor." Steven, despite being tied to a chair, looks indignant. Pissed off. As if he's preparing to lodge a formal complaint with my superiors at the university.

There's a cut on his head. It's bleeding but he smells acrid. The opposite of something I'd want in my mouth.

"I'm glad you remember me." I turn to my desk and pace over to it. There's a letter opener positioned neatly beside my large, open, notebook. It hasn't been used for centuries. I pick it up and turn it over in my hand, pressing the tip of my index finger to the end of the blade.

Steven watches me. He still doesn't look scared.

I tut and put down the knife. Then pace over to the fireplace. It's lit, as always. Crackling in the grate. Above it hangs a sword. A falcata blade I won in a card game three-hundred years ago.

Luna's boyfriend raises an eyebrow as if he's distinctly unimpressed.

The falcata is short with a curved blade. It doesn't look particularly intimidating, but it is sharp enough to split a man in half with just one slice. Especially when it's wielded by a vampire.

"You won't get away with this," he says. The upper-class lilt in his voice makes me want to behead him right now.

"I'm not sure you know who you're dealing with." I pace back to the desk and lean on it, taking my handkerchief from my pocket and using it to polish the blade so it glints in the firelight.

"You're a vampire," Steven says. "I can see that very clearly. But you have a job to hold down and you're not above the law. You're not *allowed* to kill humans. None of you are."

I examine him closely. He is not an ugly specimen. He has a square jaw and a nose that suits his face. But his hair is pale, and his soul is weak.

I can *smell* the weakness from here.

I could smell it through the window.

Only weakness makes a man treat a woman the way he treated Luna.

"That's where you're wrong, I'm afraid." I set the sword down and pour myself a glass of blood from the decanter by the window.

I allow it to stain my lips red, and enjoy the first flicker of fear on his face as he watches me lick them clean.

I pick up the blade again, my body coiling, and twitching, and shuddering as the blood takes its hold and the darkness that lives just beneath the surface of my humanity breaks free.

Steven notices the change. He is a rabbit, a deer, a small pathetic creature being stalked by something bigger and stronger.

And he knows it.

"Sadly for you, Steven, I think you'll find I am above the law."

He opens his mouth to speak but no noise comes out.

"I have ruled this city for longer than you can even begin to imagine." I wave my hands at our surroundings. "You think I've walked this planet for five hundred years and all I've achieved is to become a professor at a university museum?" I lick my fangs.

Steven swallows hard.

I stop in front of him. I lean down so I'm inches away from his pale, pathetic face. Then I whisper in his ear, "I control every supernatural creature in this city. I could make you disappear in a heartbeat, and make sure no one *ever* misses you or wonders where you've gone."

"I can turn you into smoke and dust. A figment of the imagination. A distant memory. And I will. But first..." I grip the back of his head and jerk him closer so he's staring up at me.

He whimpers.

I smile. "First, you have an apology to make."

CHAPTER 4
LUCIEN

She is trembling. I can feel her body quivering against mine as I carry her through the dark Cambridge streets.

"The box," she says, looking back over her shoulder.

"I'll retrieve it for you later."

She struggles and I drop her down into my arms instead of carrying her over my shoulder.

She looks up at me. In the darkness, her eyes shine like oil on water. I want to take her glasses off, tuck her hair behind her ear, hold her still...

I have never been this close to her, and I feel like my entire body is on fire. My muscles burn for her.

As her shirt rides up, exposing the soft flesh on her belly, and my thumb brushes against it, I almost lose my breath entirely.

In all the time I've watched her, I've never felt *this*.

"Where are you taking me?" she asks. Her arms are looped around my neck. She seems both afraid and intrigued, and I'm almost certain I can smell her arousal.

Does fear turn her on?

Or is it *me* causing this visceral reaction in her core?

Perhaps it is both.

I resist the urge to stop at the cemetery, slip my hands between her legs, and test just how wet she is with my knowing fingers. Even though the thought of seeing her gasp beneath my touch is taking over every intelligible thought in my head.

"I told you. Somewhere safe."

I move quickly, and she presses closer, holding me tighter. Humans aren't used to moving at this speed and, by the time we reach the mansion, she is even more pale than she was before.

We are on the outskirts of the city. Here, the sky is clear, and the stars shine brightly.

I set her down on the steps. She wavers for a moment, then braces herself on the door and vomits onto the threshold.

I put my hand on her back. Her skin is warm. Her breath moving fast, up and down. Her curls tease my fingertips, flowing loose over her shoulders.

When she looks up, wiping her mouth with the back of her hand, her glasses a little crooked on her nose, she shakes her head. "What the fuck was that? How do you do that?"

"I have many talents, Luna." I quirk an eyebrow at her, enjoying the fact I can make her blush when she's feeling so unsteady on her feet. "What's wrong with you?" I ask, assessing her shivering frame.

She is hugging herself and she looks suddenly exhausted. She hesitates, then frowns at me. "I have a… a pain condition. It makes me sensitive to—" She stops and puts her hands into the pockets of her cardigan. "It's hard to explain. And, frankly, boring."

Her tone surprises me. The fact I don't think I could find anything about her *boring* surprises me even more.

I nod slowly.

I have watched her long enough to know she's sick. I just never knew what kind of sick.

It's in the way she moves... as if she is always trying to stop herself from crumbling. As if she is trying to hold the pain inside, trying to stop it from overwhelming her. Eating her up.

"This way." I lead her down the corridor toward the living room. I do not, contrary to popular belief, own a coffin or have any need for one. But I do keep the mansion blissfully dark.

She will find it oppressive eventually. But, for now, it's the safest place I can keep her.

Luna follows me. She hangs back several paces as if she's not sure why she's here or why she trusts me.

If she trusts me.

The thing is, she shouldn't trust me.

If she knew... if she'd seen who I am and what I've done, she'd run.

Or would she?

I glance back. My eyes catch hers. And there it is again... that flicker of intrigue. The same flicker I saw in the shop when I very first visited her. When she suspected I was a vampire but did not *know* it for certain.

"Do you remember me?" I ask as I push open the living room door and usher her inside.

Here, the lamps are already lit, and the fire is roaring.

"Professor Lucien Thornfield," she says, hugging herself a little more tightly as I pour her a glass of whiskey.

I press it into her hands. She sniffs it and her nose wrinkles.

"You came to my shop. Twice." Her eyes flick up and meet mine.

She has no idea it is *my* shop. That I am the one who sends her books every week. That I watch her and admire her every day.

"How could I forget?" She takes a sip of whiskey, maintaining eye contact over the rim of the glass.

Is she flirting with me? Her hands are caked in her ex-boyfriend's blood. Remnants of him are on her clothes, and beneath her fingernails, and she was almost eaten by a pack of hungry vampires.

But she is not so terrified that she can't flirt?

This woman is an enigma. A code I need to crack. A delicacy I need to taste.

Without meaning to, I allow my eyes to graze her throat, the swell of her breasts, that spot where her shirt reveals the soft flesh of her side.

How I want to drag my tongue over that spot. Bite it. Tease it. Hear her whisper my name as I draw blood from it and suck, and suck.

"Are you going to explain the box?" She sits in the armchair next to the fireplace and taps her short fingernails on the whiskey glass.

"The box…" I take the chair opposite her, lean back, and cross one leg over the other. "What would you like to know?"

She frowns and adjusts her glasses on her nose. Catching sight of her blood-stained fingers, she turns her hand over, studying it in the glowing light of the fireplace.

"You killed Steven." Her voice is strangely calm.

"I have already admitted as much," I reply slowly.

Luna takes another sip of whiskey, still wincing at it. "Did he really run away with that woman?" She seems more curious that afraid, and this is not what I expected.

I do not answer her. I do not need to.

She nods in understanding. "Did she even exist?"

"She did not."

"But the police... Steven's car?" She takes a bigger sip this time.

A chuckle builds in my throat. She has no comprehension of who I am or of the hold I have on this city. "I have contacts. I can make things happen."

She leans forward, resting her forearms on her thighs. Then sits back again. She does not seem comfortable.

What must it be like to never be comfortable? To always feel *something* never *nothing*?

"So, you... kidnapped him?"

I tilt my head in answer to her question.

"Why?" She meets my eyes as she asks this.

"Because he deserved it." I stand and walk over to the fireplace, resting my glass on the mantlepiece. "He disrespected you one too many times and, unfortunately for him, I was there to witness it. In all honesty, I should have done it sooner. And for that, I apologize."

Luna raises her eyebrows. She has a defiant expression on her face, and it makes me wonder why she looked so different when she spoke to Steven. How can she stand up to a vampire and not to a weak, pathetic human? Perhaps because she can tell that while I *could* hurt her – end her life in a second if I chose – I would not. I could not *ever* cause her harm.

"You're a vampire," she says. "Why do you care what happens to me? A human?"

I'm staring into the flames, remembering the way she cried. My gut twists with displeasure, but I cannot answer her because, honestly, I have no idea why I care.

When I started watching her, she meant nothing to me.

She was a job.

Now, she is something I cannot name.

Because I have been on this forsaken planet for five-hundred years, and no one – vampire or human – has ever intrigued me the way she does.

CHAPTER 5
LUNA

He is standing by the fireplace. Shadows dance on his face, heightening his features; the strong line of his jaw, the thick dark eyebrows, the stubbled chin. His hair is jet-black with a slight curl in it. Longer than most men wear their hair, but not long enough that he'd be able to tie it back.

Shrugging off his suit jacket, Lucien tosses it onto the chair he was sitting in a moment ago. His shoulders ripple beneath his shirt, and I can't help wanting to run my thumbs under his black braces then press my palms to his broad chest.

"You are not going to answer me?" I ask, trying to sound more confident than I feel.

Thornfield tilts his head. He picks up his glass from the mantlepiece and strides back to his chair.

As he moves, my gaze flicks to his waist, then his crotch. I bite my lower lip and internally chastise myself; why the hell am I checking him out when I should be running for my life?

Why did I follow him in here?

Why am I sitting in his armchair drinking whiskey instead of screaming and fighting my way out?

I could lie to myself; claim it's because I'm afraid of him and that I know I wouldn't outrun him. But that's not true.

I am sitting here staring at him because he intrigues me.

From the second he came into the shop all that time ago, I couldn't get him out of my thoughts. I tried to. But every now and then I'd find myself daydreaming about his face. The way he looked at me. The way he said my name.

"No, Luna," he says slowly. "I am not going to answer you. But I do have something to show you if you'd like to see it."

I frown at him. Once again, my eyes dart to his crotch. This time, he notices and lets out a deep dark chuckle that trickles over my skin like warm honey.

"Not that," he says, meeting my eyes as I start to blush furiously. "Unless you'd like to see it?"

I suck in a deep breath, my cheeks pinching inwards.

Several men have hit on me since Steven disappeared. A guy I went to college with. A customer. The barista in Starbucks.

Each time, I felt a sense of panic bloom in my chest. The thought of being intimate with a man, any man, terrified me. Because how could I *ever* trust anyone again after Steven so skillfully tricked me into believing he loved me?

Yet, here, with this big muscly *vampire* – I wait for the panic to arrive and it doesn't.

"Maybe another time," Lucien mutters, still smirking. Then he walks to a large oak desk and pulls open a drawer. He pulls out a large black tablet then crosses the room and hands it to me, taking my whiskey glass and setting it down on the coffee table.

"Press play when you're ready." He sits down opposite me again, and leans forward, resting his forearms on his thighs, steepling his fingers.

He licks his fangs.

I glance down at the screen, then tap to bring it to life.

I can feel Thornfield watching me, but I cannot take my gaze from the image on the screen; a blurry still of a dark room. A man sitting in a chair.

Steven.

"What is this?" I ask, my voice barely a whisper, my heart hammering in my chest.

With fear or anticipation? I cannot tell the difference anymore.

"It is a gift," Thornfield replies.

I inhale sharply, gripping the sides of the screen so tightly my knuckles whiten and my fingers ache with the pressure.

With a shaking hand, I press play.

Steven blinks at the camera. Blood stains the side of his face, but other than that he looks unharmed. His eyes widen as a shadow moves across his face; someone else is in the room. They do not speak but I know exactly who it is.

The camera zooms in. Steven stares straight down the lens.

"Luna," he says, his tongue tripping over my name so it comes out like a choked curse word. "I have an apology to make."

He looks past the camera, and I picture Thornfield nodding at him, perhaps holding up some kind of poster with the exact words on it that Steven is supposed to be repeating.

"I treated you very badly, and you deserve better." He swallows hard. He never apologized to me once in the two years we were together, no matter what he did or how much he hurt me. All the times I went to bed crying or begged him to just be kind to me... he *never* said he was sorry.

"I am truly, very sorry for the way I treated you." Steven's hands are shaking. He looks suddenly terrified and begins to speak quicker. "I am a monster. A narcissistic, control-loving, power-hungry abuser."

There is a pause. "Say it again and mean it this time." Lucien's voice growls.

Steven clears his throat. "I am a monster. A narcissistic, control-loving, power-hungry abuser."

"Again," Lucien barks.

"I am a monster. A narcissistic, control-loving, power-hungry abuser."

"Again," Lucien commands, louder this time.

He makes Steven say those words again, and again, and again until finally... finally... it sounds as though he means them.

They break as they pass his lips. Crack and splinter and are swallowed up by his tears.

A choked sob thickens in my mouth. I close my eyes tightly. I feel the warmth of Lucien's gaze on me. But when I open my eyes again, he's no longer there. Pressure lands on my shoulders. Gentle but firm.

He is standing behind me.

One hand moves from my shoulder to my chin. He holds my face, tilting it down so I'm forced to keep watching. His lips are by my ear, his breath strangely warm and comforting on my sensitive neck.

"This is the best bit, Luna," he whispers.

Steven is crying loudly now. Big, thick tears are rolling down his pale cheeks. He shakes his head. "Please," he whispers.

Silence greets his plea. He looks back at the camera. At me.

"I don't deserve your forgiveness, Luna, and I don't deserve an easy death." His eyes widen. He is trembling. "I deserve to suffer for what I did to you." He starts to pull against the restraints on his wrists. "I deserve to suffer because a man like me will never know how to treat a woman as special as you."

A shadow falls over him.

The silhouette of Lucien's broad, muscular body appears. White shirt, black braces. Just like today. He is holding a large, curved blade in his hand.

"I'm glad you think so," Lucien says slowly. "Because I'm going to make sure you get exactly what you deserve. I'm going to make sure you can never hurt her again."

I don't think I'm breathing. I have forgotten how.

The heat of Lucien's hand on my shoulder, and on my neck, and the closeness of his body as he leans over the chair behind me... it is dizzying.

"Does watching that make you feel powerful?" he asks.

My palms and fingers are clammy. "I don't know what it makes me feel."

"Maybe you should watch it again," he whispers.

I watch the video three more times.

Each time, I notice something different. The fear in Steven's eyes. How weak he looks. How pathetic. Like a field mouse caught in the talons of a predator it can never hope to defeat.

On the second viewing, I notice that he has pissed himself and I have to fight the urge to laugh.

On the third viewing, I start to wonder how in the world I ever found him so terrifying.

How did he have so much control over me for so long? How did *this* man – this pathetic specimen of humanity – systematically destroy every flicker of joy and replace it with darkness?

Insecurity?

Doubt?

Anxiety?

Pain?

"I've seen enough." I turn the screen off and sit back in my chair.

Lucien takes his hands from my shoulders, and I instantly miss his touch. He puts the screen back in the desk drawer, then leans on the edge and folds his arms in front of his chest.

"Are you waiting for me to thank you?"

He shrugs. "If you feel thanks is appropriate, I welcome it, but I did what I did because he deserved it. Not because I was seeking your approval."

"So, this isn't some kind of weird vampire mating ritual? Kill off the boyfriend? Mail his body parts to the woman you're trying to seduce?"

For a moment, Lucien frowns at me, but then he chuckles again. It is so unexpected, it makes me smile. Dark, and delicious, his laugh is like liquid sin.

I feel myself blushing again and angle my body away from the fire as though it is the flames that are making me warm.

"I can honestly say, this is a first for me," he says, rolling up his sleeves. "And I can't imagine it's something I will be doing again."

"You've never cut off someone's penis and put it in a box before?"

Lucien tilts his head. "Oh, I've cut off all kinds of body parts. But the box was new." He taps his foot on the wooden floor. "I wanted you to know there was someone looking after you."

"You wanted me to know *you* were looking after me?"

"Not true," he says. "I did not intend for you to find out it was me, but the evening's events got away from me."

I reach for my whiskey. I have always hated whiskey, but it is cleaning the taste of the vomit from my mouth, and calming my nerves, and I need something to do with my hands.

A thick, stubborn ache is nestling between my bones, and I feel suddenly exhausted.

As if he can tell, Thornfield looks me up and down and his expression changes. "You should rest," he says firmly. "We can talk more tomorrow."

"Rest?" I almost laugh; he expects me to rest? Here? In his house?

"There are chambers you can use tonight. You'll be comfortable."

"Chambers?" This time, I do laugh. "Mansions don't have bedrooms?"

Thornfield doesn't seem to get the joke or, at least, doesn't respond to it. Instead, he stands and holds out his hand for mine.

I quirk an eyebrow at him. "And if I don't want to stay?"

"That would be unfortunate because it really is best that you do."

"I want to go." I stand up, deliberately not taking his hand. Instead, I down the rest of my drink then put the glass down firmly on the coffee table.

"I would advise you not to."

"And what if I *insist* you take me home?"

Lucien's jaw twitches. Those familiar little flecks of red appear in his eyes, and I notice his tongue moving over his fangs behind his pursed lips.

"I cannot take you home, Luna. I would prefer you stay because you understand it is best for your safety. But if you insist on leaving..." He sighs heavily. "I will do what I have to in order to keep you safe. You might not care whether you live or die, but I do."

"Which brings me back to *why* do you care?" I put my hands on my hips and close the gap between us.

"It doesn't matter why. What matters is that if you leave, those vampires will track you down and finish what they started."

"Why? I'm nothing to them." Even if for some reason I do matter, none of them stand a chance against Lucien. He proved as much when he crushed those vampires beneath his feet.

I stare at him and a look I can't decipher flits across his face. There is something more happening here; something he's hiding from me.

A long quivering moment passes between us. And then, just like that, the fight is gone. I have nothing left. Exhaustion scrapes its jagged claws down my bones and leaves me barely able to stand.

The thought of making it back across the city and then being at home alone, in the dark, with images of Steven's groveling face dancing behind my eyes… I can't even contemplate it.

"Are you staying, Luna?" Thornfield's fingers twitch at his sides as if he's resisting the urge to touch me.

I fold my arms in front of my stomach and stare into his eyes, summoning as much defiance as I can muster. "It seems I have no choice."

CHAPTER 6
LUCIEN

She is in my house. Luna. She is here.

It is the longest I have ever spent in her presence. When I visited the bookshop, our conversations were fleeting. When I watched her, I never allowed myself to watch for too long.

And now she is here.

Now I know what it is like to touch her, to be so close I can feel the pulse in her neck and the warmth of her breath. Close enough to see the way her cheeks pink when she looks at me, the way her eyes darted down my body and the way she immediately looked away. Embarrassed. Confused.

I am confused, too.

I told myself I brought her here for her protection, but as we walk through the mansion and she follows close behind me, her feet making gentle tapping sounds on the hard floor, I wonder whether that is true.

My gut tells me the vampires in the shop weren't a coincidence. That she wasn't a random choice of victim on their quest for blood. But is that because I *want* to believe she needs me?

I resist the urge to glance over my shoulder at her, even though it already feels like too many seconds have gone by since I drank in her soft features, and her pale hair, and her glistening blue eyes.

"Here." We arrive at the guest room which sits closest to my own. I push open the door and stand back so she can enter. "There are toiletries in the bathroom." I gesture to the ensuite.

She raises an eyebrow at me.

Fuck, she looks delicious when she does that. I'm not sure if it's because of the way it makes her eyes widen or because she has the nerve to chastise me with just a glance, but I can't get enough of it.

She nudges the bathroom door open and takes in the toothbrush, the women's razor, and the coconut shampoo. Her shampoo. The one she uses to make her hair smell so good I want to bury myself in the scent of it.

"Did you know you were going to bring me here tonight?" she asks, folding her arms in front of her stomach.

I hate it when she does that; as if she's trying to hide the most delicious parts of herself. I want to tug her arms down by her sides and demand she never does it again.

But I can't do that.

Not yet.

Not until she is mine.

In that moment – that exact moment – I realize that no matter what the circumstances that brought her here, this is what I've always wanted since the moment I first saw her.

To make her mine.

"No, I did not." I lean past her and tug the bathroom door closed. I feel her breath hitch as my body moves closer to her.

"Then you have a lot of female guests staying here?" she asks.

"No, I do not." I lean on the doorframe, arm positioned above her so she is sheltered beneath it.

Now, she lowers her arms. She drops them to her sides and grips the frame. Her pelvis tilts toward me. She doesn't even know she's doing it, but her body tells me things she does not.

"Who was the queen?"

The question catches me off guard. I was lost in the vibration of heat between us, but now I stand back, lace my fingers behind my back and pace away from her.

"That doesn't concern you." I don't look back. I stand in the doorway, facing the dark hallway instead of her brightness.

"I think it does. I think it has to do with why I'm here."

"It is a business matter." I wrap my fingers around the handle. "And something you are best staying away from."

I wait a beat longer than I should. Curious to see whether she will challenge me more. But then I feel her sigh. Her energy shifts. I hear her sit down on the edge of the bed. Is she resting her head in her hands? Is she rubbing her aching back?

"Get some rest, Luna. We will talk tomorrow."

I close the door and take a key from the hook on the wall beside it.

Then I lock her in.

∼

It takes me only a few seconds to reach my office. Moving at speed isn't something I like to do unless there is true urgency, but knowing Luna is here, locked in my house, is doing something to the instincts I usually keep under control.

I feel like I've consumed some particularly powerful blood, and yet I have drunk nothing all day. My muscles are tight and alert. I want to run, jump, climb. Use the power that I restrain and keep buried.

I want to feed.

It has been months since I fed on a human. Occasionally, I have my men bring me a donor. Never females, always males. I make them sit in the armchair by the fireplace in my office, and I feed from their neck. Standing behind them. I slide my hands down their chest, beneath their shirt. I feel their breathing change as I drink, their pulse quickens, and their blood becomes more acidic as the adrenaline in their body starts to run riot.

I take them to the brink. To the point where they think I might be about to end them for good.

And then I let them go.

I have often wondered whether it is my way of proving to myself I still have control. That the reason I am so powerful, and can command this godforsaken city, is because I am better than the rest of the vampires who live here.

I don't need the rush of a feeding session.

I can live without it.

I can fight the animal inside me.

I can control the demon.

Right now, though? For the first time in a long time, I think I would struggle to control myself if a thick, throbbing vein was offered to me.

I slam the office door closed, open up the computer and reach for the flask in my desk drawer. The good stuff. Aged but not fermented; I do not do drugs. Never have. And I don't know a single vampire who takes Fermented Human Blood who has kept hold of their sanity.

I take a long, thirsty drink.

The crimson liquid coats my teeth, and gums, and slides exquisitely down my throat.

I sit down at the desk and type in my password. The bank of hidden cameras appears on screen. Twenty of them. I navigate past the bookshop and the streets surrounding it. I move past the cameras positioned outside Luna's house, and the ones that line her journey to work. I keep going until I find the one I'm looking for.

The one that shows her sitting on the edge of the large four-poster bed in my bedroom.

In my house.

I sigh and lean back in my chair, relief flooding through me, chasing the thrill of her blood.

She is safe.

I have her.

She is safe.

When she stands and begins to pace back and forth, bracing her hands on her lower back, I force myself to close the feed and instead open up the recordings from the past twenty-four hours.

The bookshop. I need to see what happened when she opened the box.

The glow of the monitor casts eerie shadows across my face as I lean in, captivated by Luna's movements. My eyes, far sharper than a human's, catch every subtle shift in her expression as she sets the box down on the countertop.

As she traces the carvings on the lid, I frown and lean closer.

I hit pause, skip back a few seconds, then play it again.

Fuck.

I was right.

She is staring at the box, her breath is quickening, and all around her... the shadows that live in the crevices between the bookshelves, and beneath the desk, and in the hidden corners of the room, seem to respond to her touch.

She does not see them, but I do.

They stretch and curl in ways that defy natural light.

My breath catches. I have suspected it for so long... but I thought I was confusing my obsession with reality.

I thought I had come to believe she was special because I found her so irresistible.

But what if I was right?

When Luna finally opens the box, the room around her darkens, as if the very night is drawn to her presence. The shadows coalesce, forming a velvety cocoon around her. It's subtle, almost imperceptible to mortal eyes, but to me, it's unmistakable.

I watch, mesmerized, as she examines the contents of the box. Her hands are steady now. There's a strength in her movements that I've longed to see. The same strength that shimmered on her skin when she watched the video of her tormentor being tormented.

It makes my heart swell with pride.

Oh, how I wish she could see how strong she is.

The moment she realizes what — who — the parts belong to, I lick my lips. Will this be the catalyst? The shadows pulse. A laugh bubbles up from her chest – a sound of relief, of liberation.

My cold heart swells with affection. She understands. She sees the gift for what it is – freedom from the man who made her life a living death.

As she lifts out Steven's tongue, the shadows grow denser, absorbing the flickering light of the bookshop. They move with purpose now, as if Luna's emotions are giving them form and direction. It is breathtaking to behold.

But then she looks up. The door opens.

I pause again and skip back. This time, I pay attention to the window and try to see past the shopfront into the street.

A figure moves into view.

More than one.

They were watching her.

I skip back further, to before the box arrived.

Luna moves slowly around the shop, cleaning up, getting ready to close. I try not to watch her and focus on the window instead.

There, the same figure.

They were watching her before the box was delivered. Which means they were not drawn to her by the scent of Steven's blood.

I clench my fist and slam it so hard onto the desk that it leaves a large imprint in the shape of my knuckles.

"Fuck..."

For the first time in my many centuries on earth, I did not want to be right.

I grab my phone and raise it to my ear. It rings twice then...

"Kim?"

The only human I trust, apart from Luna, answers with sleep in his voice and irritation in his breath. "The fuck time do you call this, Lucien? We had a deal. No more night jobs. I'm your daytime guy. You have your vampire henchmen for nighttime."

"I need you for this."

I picture him putting on his glasses and pinching his nose, his stupidly floppy hair falling over his eyes. "For what?"

"Just get here. Now. It's nearly morning."

"For *what* Lucien?"

My jaw tics. "It's about the Covenant."

There is a long pause. Kim's breathing changes, and when he speaks again his tone is more urgent. "I'll be there as soon as I can."

CHAPTER 7
LUNA

The sound of the key turning in the lock makes my heart twist violently. I can't move. All I can do is stare at the place where, a moment ago, Lucien Thornfield stood baring his fangs at me.

Does he really expect me to believe he's brought me here for my protection?

Okay, yes, he saved me in the bookshop. But he was *watching* me. He kidnapped my ex-boyfriend. He cut off Steven's body parts and mailed them to me with a note.

What did the note say?

I'll always protect you.

For a while, when I was watching that video of Steven, and Thornfield was standing behind me smelling like sin and seduction, I forgot what he really is.

I listened to the heat humming on my skin instead of the facts.

And the fact is; he's a vampire.

He's a sick, twisted, vampire stalker and who knows what he'll do to me if he keeps me here.

What does he want? A vampire bride? A human sex slave?

I mean, sure, he's smoking hot. Like, the kind of hot that should only exist in movies because it's not fair for something *that* perfectly muscular and chiseled and smoldering to exist in real life.

But he's a vampire.

He drinks blood to sustain himself.

And now he has me, a living, breathing, blood supply locked up in his house.

I leave the bed and start to pace back and forth, bracing my hands on my lower back. Anxiety and adrenaline are turning to gristle in my muscles. Gristle that grates, and rubs, and becomes pain that I won't be able to shift.

Instinctively, I reach for my bag then realize I don't have it; it's back at the shop. And so are my pain meds.

Fuck.

Fuck, fuck, fuck.

I try not to let the overwhelming sense of panic take over. I try to think clearly, but I have no idea whether I'm more terrified of going cold turkey on my meds or of what Lucien Thornfield plans to do with me.

To me.

I stride over to the door and rattle the handle. Of course, it's no use. The door is locked.

I close my eyes and see the video of Steven. His face.

Pleasure and revulsion converge in the pit of my stomach.

Did I enjoy seeing him like that?

I turn around and lean my back against the door, the cool wood making me shiver through my sweater.

Wrapping my arms around my waist, I slide down so I'm sitting on the floor. I try to breathe slowly, purposefully, in and out, in and out. I adjust my glasses on the bridge of my nose. I do the square trick. Picture forming all for sides as I inhale and exhale. Try to make each breath as long as the last.

I hug myself and rub my upper arms, then tap my chest. All tricks I've learned over the years to soothe myself when my nervous system becomes completely dysregulated.

Usually, one of them works. Something shifts and I start to feel calmer. Warmer. Safer.

Here, tonight, my tricks do nothing.

My entire body feels too alive, too alert, too switched on. And I can't think straight.

There was a time when Steven took my medication from me. He told me it wasn't helping, and that the doctors had given it to me because they didn't know what else to do.

"If it was a real illness, it would show up on blood tests, Luna."

"But they said it's to do with my nervous system..."

He rolled his eyes and snatched the pills out of my hand. "ME, Chronic Fatigue, Fibro-whatever... they're all the same. Labels made up by doctors because they have to say *something* to placate their needy patients." He tapped my forehead. Hard. "It's all up here, my love. See what happens if you stop them. I'll wager it makes no difference at all." He kissed my forehead this time. "Trust me."

After a week of being barely able to get out of bed, and fearing I'd lose my job because I'd ignored my boss's emails, hadn't showed up for work, and the bookshop had been closed all week, I dragged myself to the doctors and told them I'd lost my meds so had decided to see if I could cope without them.

They gave me a strict talking to and a new prescription, with instructions *never* to just quit like that again.

After that, I hid them from him. I kept them at work, in my desk drawer, and took them only on days I was in the shop. It made Sundays and holidays hard, but Steven just assumed that was because I was tired from work.

Before he disappeared, he'd been trying to convince me to give up my job. Stay home. Make life easy on myself because clearly I was too weak to hold down even the most non-taxing of careers.

Thinking of the shop, and the smell of the old books, and the sense of peace that washes over me every time I walk through the door and hear the bell ringing, makes a lump form in my throat.

With Steven gone, I had a glimpse of a life I thought I might live. One where I could take control of my own destiny. Grow stronger, and brighter. Maybe even wear heels again.

Now, I'm here. Trapped in a creepy old mansion with a creature that could kill me in a fraction of a second.

And there is no way in hell I'll be strong enough to escape him; I couldn't fight back even if I wanted to.

I'm weak, and he knows it.

After all, he's been watching me, hasn't he?

How long for, I have no idea. Did it start after his first visit to the bookshop? Was I too friendly? Or was he following me before that?

He says he brought me here to protect me. But he also said he'd force me to stay if I tried to leave.

I bite my lower lip. I cannot cry. Not here, not now.

Think, Luna. Think.

I brace my hand on the door and stand up slowly. My body seems to preemptively hurt. I took my pills this morning; I shouldn't be suffering this much already.

But I can't just lie down and accept the fate Lucien has in store for me. I have to fight. For once in my life, I have to fight back. And if I can't use my strength, I'll have to use the one thing I do have: my brains.

He might be incredibly good looking. He might make my mind

and my body race in a way that no one ever has, and I might *feel* like I can trust him.

But I learned a long time ago that I can't trust my feelings.

My head is telling me to get out. So, that's what I'm going to do.

I am *not* going to be the girl who convinces herself a vampire won't hurt her just because he has a sexy smile or an intoxicating laugh or muscles for days.

I stand in the center of the room and examine my surroundings. A large four poster bed, which looks like something from a period drama. White, billowy drapes, deep red blankets, and pillows that are temptingly fluffy.

There are wooden floors, and a large rug.

Dark walls. It's hard to tell exactly what color they are because the only light is candlelight, which, honestly, is a bit of a cliche.

Why couldn't he have had a suave, modern, minimalist place? Polished concrete floors and expansive glass windows?

I turn around slowly, taking in all four walls.

There are no windows here. Not one. Just huge, ugly paintings. One of a polar bear, standing on its haunches, with a bright white light surrounding it.

A couple showing old fashioned portraits of people I assume are Thornfield's relatives.

And a phoenix. A glittering, red and gold and orange phoenix.

This one intrigues me. It is in the same, old, gilded frame as the others. But it looks more modern. The brushstrokes are more liberal, more free. The paint thicker. I press my index finger to the canvas, half expecting Thornfield to appear behind me and tell me off for touching.

I am staring at the initials scrawled in the corner of the canvas, *LT,* when I notice a small freckle of light on the wall beside the frame.

LUNA

I move sideways.

It's more than a freckle.

It's a long, thin sliver of light.

And it's coming from behind the painting.

What time is it? Could it be sunrise already?

I stretch my arms wide, and grab hold of the side of the frame. It is huge, and thick, and heavy, and my arms are already straining with the effort of stretching so wide.

With every ounce of strength I possess, I groan loudly as I lift it up, freeing it from its hanging, then pull it away from the wall.

As soon as I'm holding all of the painting's weight, I stumble. I turn around and stagger toward the bed before letting it fall.

It lands with a soft thud.

And daylight floods the room.

When I turn around, rubbing my arms, breathing heavily, I blink and shield my eyes.

The painting was hiding a window, and beyond the window, the sun is rising against a bright pink sky.

This time, I do let myself cry.

Because maybe I just found my way out of here.

CHAPTER 8

KIM

The first time I came to Lucien's mansion, I could barely bring myself to step over the threshold. The place is so thick with dark supernatural energy that I almost choked on it.

When I first started hunting demons, and became aware of my powers, I would have run screaming from a place like this. But these days, things are different. I'm starting to embrace who I am, and instead of repelling me or congealing like toxic waste in my veins, the darkness calls to me.

Pulls me closer.

Like it is trying to seduce me but doesn't realize I'm tricking it into a false sense of security. Allowing it to envelop me tighter and tighter until... SNAP.

I destroy it.

This mainly applies to demons, not vampires.

Part of my *deal* with Lucien is that the vamps are left largely alone. Not just because there's debate about whether or not they are demons, but because he claims to have them under control.

I am not so sure. Especially lately. The past few months, it hasn't been the demons causing havoc in the city; it has been rogue vampires. And his usual methods of keeping them on their best behavior don't seem to be working.

I press the buzzer next to the large, wrought iron gates. Trent answers. He's a slimy bastard. A werewolf, which surprises me because historically Thornfield hasn't been able to abide werewolves.

Apparently, though, Trent is different. He rescued him as a pup. Indoctrinated him into the Firm.

Honestly, I still don't really understand all this stuff.

"What do you want?" Trent barks down the speaker.

"Thornfield sent for me."

"He didn't tell me."

"He doesn't tell you everything." I roll my eyes, stifling a yawn. It's too early and I'm too grouchy for this sort of back and forth. Trent hates that Lucien has brought me into his inner circle when we've only known each other a short while. I hate that Trent exists.

It is a mutually egregious relationship.

Huffing at me, Trent unlocks the gates. They swing open, exposing a long straight driveway lined by silver birch trees. A strange mist lingers between them. Above, the sun is starting to rise. It is going to be the kind of cold, crisp winter's day that makes England look peaceful and majestic.

I get back into the car and drive through slowly.

Up ahead, the mansion looms into view. Thornfield tells me it has been in his family for centuries. Perhaps there was a time when a larger nest of vampires lived here, but now it is just him. His staff don't even live here. He has a few security guys, and girls, and a gardener. That's it. Apart from me, I suppose.

None of us live on site. He calls us if he needs us, and we come running.

That's the deal with Thornfield.

I pass the expansive lawn. A fountain, big box hedges, landscaped flower beds. Jogging up the stone steps to the front door, I shiver. There is something different in the air today.

The mansion's energy is usually thick and black and toxic – the remnants of centuries of dark, shady shit that has gone down here. Evil. If 'evil' is a real thing.

Today, something else shimmers beneath it. I close my eyes and try to latch onto the sensation. It is not demonic energy. Not vampire either.

It has no color.

It just feels like... power.

It hits me in the chest and knocks the breath from my lungs. I stumble backward, and I'm steadying myself on a nearby concrete pillar when the door swings open. Trent greets me with his arms folded in front of his skinny chest. He's wearing a jet-black suit, as if he is auditioning for the role of 'mafia henchman' in a movie, and he stinks of dog.

He curls his lip at me in a wolfish grin.

Clearly, he's not long returned from a shift. I almost wish he'd stayed that way; he's more palatable when he looks cute.

"He's in his office." Trent deliberately blocks the doorway for a moment longer than necessary. I don't push past him, just wait casually for him to move. All the while, still feeling the throb of whatever new energy has settled in this place.

"What's been happening?" I ask as Trent follows me down the corridor.

He frowns.

"Sounded urgent."

Trent shrugs. Clearly, he has no idea what's been going on,

but wants to pretend he does. "I'm sure he'll explain when he sees you," is the best response he can manage.

Poor, stupid bastard.

When I knock on the door to Thornfield's study, he answers immediately, and I find him with his hands braced on the windowsill. Shutters closed. Fire blaring. His shoulders are hunched and he's breathing heavily. He doesn't turn around to face me but growls, "Trent, this doesn't concern you."

"But—"

"Leave," he commands.

I try not to smirk. Instead, I offer Trent an exaggerated look of *sorry, mate*, and watch him stalk off down the hallway.

When he's out of sight, I close the door and walk over to the window. Lucien remains stock still, staring down at his knuckles, which are white with pressure. There is blood on his chin. I glance at the desk and notice the flask of blood. Good news because it means he hasn't fed on an actual human.

"Well?" I ask, folding my arms. "You got me out of bed at the crack of dawn. What's happening? Has the Covenant surfaced?"

There is a quivering pause and then Thornfield turns around. His eyes are almost pitch black and small crimson flecks dance on their surface.

"Not the Covenant, no. Something much bigger than that..."

"All right, do you want to stop talking like a cryptic crime lord in a superhero movie and just tell me what's happening? Or are we going to do ominous soundbites all morning? Because, honestly, Thornfield, I'm knackered. I was out tracking a Marling demon until two a.m. and..."

"Do you remember me telling you about Luna?"

I stifle a laugh. Of course, I remember. He doesn't fucking shut up about her. And when he decided to off her boyfriend, who got called for cleanup duty?

That one pissed me off; I've *never* cleaned up after a human kill before. When Thornfield explained what the guy had done, what kind of man he was, I saw why he'd done it. But I still wasn't happy he'd gotten me involved in something that could have resulted in actual jail time.

"She's here." Thornfield folds his arms and leans back on the windowsill, facing the room but looking at me.

"Here?" I glance around his study, half expecting her to jump out from under the desk.

Thornfield nods. "There was an incident at the bookshop last night." He paces over to the desk and turns the computer screen toward me, then presses play on a video. For a moment, my breath hitches. My skin starts to tingle.

I look away, but Thornfield growls at me to watch, so I force my gaze back to the screen.

Fuck.

She looks like Sarah.

If I didn't know my wife was dead, I'd think I was watching her. Living, breathing, moving.

I peer at the screen, moving closer.

She has Sarah's eyes, her curls, her curves. She moves differently though. As I watch, I understand that. The way her hips sway, the shape of her ass, the clothes she's wearing.

She is not Sarah.

But she could be.

Thornfield is staring at me. "What's wrong with you? You look pale?"

I shake my head and point at the screen. "You have access to the security cameras where she works?"

"Clearly," Thornfield replies dryly.

"Okay, so what am I looking at?"

"Just watch."

He points again at the screen.

Luna — that's her name, I remind myself — is opening a package. Her movements are careful, almost reverent. As she lifts out a wooden box, I notice something odd. The shadows in the bookshop seem to shift, moving in ways that don't align with the light sources I can see.

My skin prickles. This is more than just poor video quality or tricks of the light.

Luna opens the box, and I brace myself because it is clear that whatever is inside is significant. She dips in her hand then pulls it out again. This time, it's covered in blood.

"What's in the box, Lucien?"

Thornfield arches a thick dark eyebrow at me. "Remember Steven?"

"The boyfriend..." I trail off. "He's...?"

"Parts of him." Thornfield's lip twitches into a satisfied smile.

Sick mother fucker. He *mailed* her the ex-boyfriend's body parts?

"Keep watching." Thornfield taps the screen.

Luna is staring into the box. But instead of recoiling in horror, she seems fascinated. Empowered, even. And around her, the shadows in the room grow darker, swirling, moving.

"Is she...?"

I watch as Luna examines the contents of the box. Her hands should be shaking - anyone's would be — but they're steady. Strong. There's a moment where she laughs, and the sound seems to make the very air around her vibrate.

The shadows are still moving. They pulse and writhe, responding to her emotions. It's subtle, but unmistakable to someone who's seen as much supernatural shit as I have.

"She's controlling them," I mutter, more to myself than to

Thornfield. "The shadows. She's not even aware she's doing it, is she?"

Thornfield doesn't answer, but his silence is confirmation enough.

He stops the clip and I step back from the screen, running a hand through my hair. "Okay, so she's got some kind of power. Shadow magick? But she's human?"

I turn to face Thornfield, my mind racing. This woman, whoever she is, is clearly more than just some human Thornfield's obsessed with. She's powerful, potentially dangerous, and completely unaware of what she can do.

"Precisely."

"You don't think...?"

Thornfield meets my eyes. "I need you to go to the bookshop. Clean up. Retrieve the box and tell me what you sense while you're there. You saw what I saw... you saw the shadows moving. If she has shadow magick..."

"That's a bit of a stretch, Lucien. I know you're convinced the Covenant is real but—"

"It *is* real." Thornfield bares his fangs. Once upon a time, that would have intimidated me. But not now.

I raise my palms and speak slowly. "Alright. I'll go."

I cross to the door. I need to clear my head. If she's here, and she really can do shadow magick, she could be the reason the energy around the mansion has shifted. *She* could be the power I'm feeling. But if Thornfield knows that, I'm not sure whether he'll want to protect her or own her.

∼

As soon as I unlock the door to the bookshop, the unmistakable stench of rapidly rotting vampire corpses hits me smack bang in the face. My stomach turns, and I slam my hand over my nose and mouth, but I force myself to step inside.

Since the Queen died, and I somehow got hooked up with Lucien Thornfield — Cambridge Mafia Supremo — I've spent more time cleaning up after him than I have hunting demons. Which is *supposed* to be my job.

Thornfield argues that they are the same thing.

I've seen this stuff before, but this particular scene is even more grim than I anticipated.

Putrid flesh sloughs off the vampires' bones, leaving slimy piles on the hardwood floor. Dark blood oozes and congeals into tacky pools. I've seen a lot of disturbing things since becoming a demon hunter, but this is next level disgusting.

I retrieve cleaning supplies from the back room, holding my breath against the overpowering reek of decay. As I mop and disinfect, nausea ripples through me.

Is that a fucking *tongue* on the floor?

I pick it up with my thumb and forefinger and drop it into the bucket.

I can't believe Lucien is making me do this solo. He could have at least made Trent tag along.

But maybe he doesn't want Trent to know about Luna.

Maybe, somehow, I have become Thornfield's most trusted person.

As I clean, my mind wanders to Luna. Poor girl. I can't imagine the trauma she's endured — losing her boyfriend, only to have his dismembered corpse delivered to her work. And now she's trapped in Lucien's mansion, at the mercy of an obsessive vampire who claims he wants to protect her.

Right now, I think I believe him.

If it turns out he's right and Luna has something to do with the Covenant... well, who the hell knows whether he'll stay chivalrous.

I stop and look around for the box. It was on the countertop, but now all that remains is a stack of blood-stained papers. No box.

I check under the counter, all the dark corners of the room.

It is not here.

Which means Thornfield will be extra pissed.

I glance up in the direction of the hidden security camera in case he's watching and offer an exaggerated shrug. Then I return to scooping up bits of dead vampire.

I'm scrubbing coagulated blood off the skirting boards when the hairs on my arms and neck start to prickle.

I whirl around, reaching for the blade I keep on my belt, but see nothing. There is a shift in energy, but it is not the energy I felt at the mansion.

Something evil was here... or still is.

Heart pounding, I extend my senses, trying to pinpoint the source of the malevolent aura. As I reach further into the ether, it becomes thick and cloying, seeping from the very walls.

I've never encountered anything this potent.

I start to cough, choking on the acrid taste of it.

Whatever this is, it's ancient... and hungry.

It presses down on me, announcing its presence. Imprinting itself on my skin.

I close my eyes and the mop clatters from my hand. Pain throbs in my temples.

And then it is gone.

Just like that.

I open my eyes again, panting, struggling for breath.

Unnerved, I continue cleaning with renewed urgency.

I need to get the fuck out of here.

Every creak and groan of the old building sets my nerves on edge, and I can't shake the sensation of being watched, stalked by an unseen predator. But not via the security cameras.

I feel as though something is *here*.

As I tie off another trash bag bulging with putrid remains, a floorboard behind me creaks. I spin around, blade drawn, only to find myself face to face with my own reflection in an antique mirror. Jesus. Get it together, Kim.

But then, in the mirror's tarnished surface, I glimpse a flicker of movement. A shadow where there shouldn't be one.

Ice floods my veins as I stare into the glass. But the harder I focus, the more distorted my reflection becomes, warping into a nightmarish caricature with hollow, bottomless eyes and a leering gash of a mouth.

Fuck this.

I lunge for the mirror, intent on smashing it to pieces. But before my hand makes contact, an invisible force slams into my chest, hurling me backwards. I hit the floor hard, breath knocked from my lungs. The demonic aura intensifies, pressing down on me like a physical weight, drowning me in darkness.

Gasping, I claw my way upright, gripping my blade in sweat-slick hands. But the oppressive energy dissipates as quickly as it appeared, leaving me alone and shaking amid the gore-streaked shelves.

What the actual fuck just happened?

I look back in the direction of the hidden camera, praying Thornfield hasn't been watching. Because whatever just happened, I need to figure out whether he can be trusted with it before I tell him.

I need to know what he'll do to the girl. What she means to him.

I need to know if Luna is safe with Lucien Thornfield.

CHAPTER 9
LUNA

I press my palms to the window and stare out at the brightening sky.

How is it sunrise already? Were we talking for that long?

The glass is cool against my slightly clammy palms, and the sensation calms me a little. Until I look down.

The room he's keeping me in is, of course, on the top floor.

Outside, there is a huge expanse of lawn and a long, sprawling driveway. At the end of it, tall black wrought-iron gates.

Even if I, somehow, made it down the outside of the building, how would I actually get out of the grounds? Surely, a guy like Thornfield will have dogs, or bodyguards or – hell – werewolves waiting to grab me and drag me back inside.

I shake my arms, splaying my fingers at my sides to release some tension. I swallow hard, fear beating a hard heavy rhythm against my ribs.

I look back at the door.

The next time Lucien Thornfield walks through it, he might not just want to talk to me. He might want something else.

Everything else.

As I think about his huge, muscular frame, my treacherous stomach tightens with a quiver of intrigue.

Sex with Steven was... perfunctory at best and awful at worst.

Dark room. Him on top. Eyes closed. Lying still.

Is there a part of me that wants to know what might happen if I choose to stay and let Lucien destroy me?

I'd be lying if I said no.

But the biting? The drinking my blood and draining me dry?

Not so much into that.

I turn back to the window and inhale deeply. Looks like I only have one option.

This time, after flexing my fingers, I try the latch on the window. Of course, it doesn't move. But the glass doesn't look thick. There is air coming in from tiny gaps in the frame.

I raise my arm, thinking about smashing the glass with my elbow. Then think again; that's going to *hurt*.

Instead, I go for the candlestick on the sideboard.

See, if he'd gone minimalist, this wouldn't be happening. It would be all reinforced glass and no huge, heavy objects to pierce it with.

The candlestick really is heavy. I weigh it up and down in my hand. I stare at the glass. I've done this before. Not with a candlestick. With my foot.

I slam my eyes closed and memories that usually only haunt me at night barrel into my mind. Being upside down, being trapped. The sound of the radio still blaring. The scent of the blood. The spiderweb crack on the windscreen. Pushing it with my foot. My shoe gone. Why was it gone?

Kicking, and kicking, and screaming until it shattered.

A cold sweat has broken out on my forehead, and in the small of my back. Nausea swells in my throat. I grip the candlestick tighter. My knuckles whiten with the pressure. I know what sound it's going to make when it makes contact with the glass. I just don't know what will happen inside my head when I hear it.

I don't know if it will bounce off, repelled by adrenaline and the need to get the fuck out of here. Or if it will bury deep inside my skull and find the places where it can hurt me the most, and leave me sobbing on the floor.

Whatever is about to happen, I have no choice.

I have to confront it or I will be stuck here forever.

With him.

Forever… or until he ends me.

I lift the candlestick with one shaking arm. It is so heavy my muscles burn. I pull my arm back, take a deep breath, then hurl it at the window.

The glass is stronger than I thought.

It splinters. A shard falls free, then another, but some remain attached. Clinging to the edges of the frame like jagged teeth. Jaws waiting to swallow me.

No.

Spit me out.

I am leaving this place.

Pulling my cardigan down over my hand, I brush the stubborn remaining shards from the window. Some fall in, some fall out.

I look down, trying to follow the path of the ones that have fallen to the ground. But I'm too high up; I cannot see or hear them land.

Gripping the top of the frame, I haul myself up so I'm standing on the sill. I hold on tightly, digging my fingernails into the flaky wood.

My legs feel weak and shaky. I know shouldn't look down, but I do. And I feel like I'm standing on the edge of a cliff. Below, the tall uncut grass sways in the breeze. An ocean of green waiting to swallow me up if I fall.

Except, it will not swallow me. I will meet it, and I will break.

I close my eyes. The rising sun is warm on my face. I can't jump. I have to climb, but I have no idea how to do that.

Still holding onto the frame, I look left and right, examining the sides of the building. From the sill, there is a small rim of protruding brick that runs along the outside of the building. Maybe four feet from where I'm standing, there is a drainpipe.

I am *not* the sort of person who can climb down a building clinging onto a drainpipe. I'm too heavy, for starters.

I have visions of the drainpipe creaking and groaning and breaking away from the building, sending me falling into the large oak tree opposite.

The tree...

Its branches are large and thick and bare; it is too early in the year for it to have grown lush and green. But some of them protrude out toward the building. Are they close enough to grab hold of? If I jump?

I think back to the days when I used to take gymnastics lessons. Before the accident. Before I stopped wearing heels and being able to use my body the way I wanted to use it.

Back then, I could probably have made it. Just.

Now?

I am tapping my foot nervously on the sill, hanging on, looking from the drainpipe to the tree when I hear the one thing that could terrify me even more than the thought of falling to my death; the door.

The bedroom door.

Opening.

I spin around, wavering, grabbing the side of the frame instead of the top. My palm meets with a stray splinter of glass, piercing it, hard. I cry out, wobble again, and feel as if I'm teetering backward.

In the dark doorway, Lucien stares at me with inky black eyes. His sleeves are rolled up. He's still wearing his shirt and braces. He fills the doorframe, but he doesn't move.

Extending all the way up to the toes of his polished, black shoes is a beam of light. Wide, and bright. He rolls his tongue around his mouth, moistening his fangs behind his lips.

He tilts his head. "Where are you going, Luna?"

"Away from here." I try to sound stronger than I feel.

A small smile snags at the corner of his mouth, and I find it instantly infuriating.

"You don't think I mean it?" I turn back around, looking away from him toward the tree instead. Because somehow, looking at him is making it harder to want to go.

"Oh, I believe you mean it." He moves. I can feel it. I glance back and watch him stepping around the large shaft of light. Will he turn to ash if it touches him? "I'm just not sure you're capable of such a large jump."

Again, indignation flares in my gut.

"Fuck you," I mutter.

Then, without thinking, without even pausing for breath, I jump.

My arms flail in front of me, my fingers stretch, my legs peddle hilariously as if I'm trying to walk on thin air. My fingertips brush the nearest branch, but it's small and weak, like me, and it won't hold me. I know it won't.

Everything moves fast and slow at the same time.

I cry out. I'm falling.

And then I'm not.

He has hold of me. His arms are around my waist. He is

holding me with one hand and the thickest upper branch of the tree with his other. And he is smoking.

Not a cigar.

His *body* is smoking. The skin on his exposed forearm starts to blister and crack. He growls loudly, then in one swift motion hauls us both up onto the branch. He scoops me into his arms, tossing me onto his shoulder like he did in the bookshop, balancing on the branch as if he's some kind of fucking acrobat.

In one leap, we are back inside, tumbling onto the floor.

As he drops me, he scrambles away from the light like a wounded animal. He is behind the bed, hiding in shadow. He stands, smoke still simmering on the surface of his skin.

His arms and face and neck are blistered and red. He pushes past me into the light again, grabs the painting, and slams it back onto its fixings so hard the wall behind it gains a hairline fracture.

I am standing in the corner of the room, pressed up against the wall, barely able to breathe.

When he turns around, the room now dark again and only lit by candles, he is glaring at me with a look that makes me want to run for my life.

He paces toward me. A tiger approaching its prey.

Then he grabs me. He jerks my arm up between us and with his gaze fixed on mine, he says, "Luna?"

"Yes," My reply comes out as barely more than a whisper.

"You're bleeding."

"I cut my hand on the glass."

His eyes travel from my face to my hand, and I swear little flecks of red appear in them when he stares at the crimson droplets running down my arm.

"I told you it is not safe out there," he murmurs.

When his eyes meet mine again, I shake my head and try to

pull away from him. But he doesn't let me go. "Stop pretending you're trying to protect me. I've seen the way you look at me."

He smiles, and a flutter of warmth settles in my belly. "You are bleeding onto my shirt, what do you expect?"

"I don't mean now." I tilt my chin up, try to look like I'm perfectly confident standing up to someone who could end my life at any second. "I mean always. When you appeared in the bookshop. When you brought me here." I inhale sharply, my breath swelling in my chest. "When you look at me it's like…"

"Like what, Luna?"

"Like you're trying to decide whether you want to drink from me or fuck me."

Did I just say that? Why the hell did I just say that?

Lucien tweaks his index finger beneath my chin, then closes the gap between us. One hand is on my waist. The other is holding my wrist, my blood slowly pooling in my palm and dripping down onto his fingers. He lets me go and raises his fingers to his mouth.

Still staring at me, wiping my blood onto his lips, he says, "What if I want to do both?"

CHAPTER 10
LUNA

My entire body feels like it's on fire. Like if he stares at me a moment longer, my skin will start to burn the way his did when it was touched by the sunlight.

I stare at my blood on his lips. I expect him to lick them clean. Instead, he leans in and brushes my hair away from my neck.

As his fingertips make contact with my skin, a sigh escapes my mouth. I feel my body tilting toward him, trying to close the space between us. His lips meet my skin. They are damp, still coated with my blood, and as he trails a line of kisses down my throat, I know he is leaving a trail of scarlet with his mouth.

He lifts his head and stares at me. I'm breathing hard, and fast. My chest rising and falling, and making my breasts even more noticeable beneath my cardigan.

With one expert finger, he flicks open the top button, then the next.

Then he uses the same finger to make me tilt my head back, and he licks the blood from my skin. One, long, torturous movement of his tongue that sends shivers of arousal skittering down the front of my body. Between my breasts, over my stomach, to settle between my legs.

"If I told you to stop, would you?" I meet his eyes.

I don't know whether I expect him to tell me the truth. But when he says, "Yes," I believe him.

His hand moves to my waist and unfastens my jeans. He rests his fingers on the waistline of my panties and seems to square his shoulders so he's taller and bigger, and towering over me.

"Do you want me to stop?" His fingers slip lower but stay on top of the fabric.

I stumble backward a little, leaning on the dresser. He moves with me, his palm now resting between my legs, cupping my pussy, applying just the smallest amount of pressure.

"I'll ask you again. Do you want me to stop?" His other hand slides my cardigan from my shoulders. It falls to the floor, leaving me in just my white tank top, jeans open.

My hands move instinctively to my belly, but he catches my wrist. Then he lifts my shirt, bends down, and kisses my stomach. A long, lingering kiss.

No one has ever kissed me there before.

"No," I whisper. "I don't want you to stop."

He kisses me again, gently grazing the soft skin around my bellybutton with his teeth.

A small, kitten-like murmur escapes my lips, and I find myself tilting my pelvis so I'm pressing down onto his palm.

"So warm," he murmurs, lifting his gaze to stare up at me. "Does that mean you're getting wet for me, Luna?"

I can't answer him. Instead, I just stare.

He moves his lips to the side of my stomach, just above my waist, and inhales deeply. He sighs, nips at my flesh with gentle teeth, then kisses me. "Do you know how many times I have dreamed of kissing this spot?" he growls.

I still cannot answer.

When he takes his hand away from my pussy, I almost whimper.

But then he tugs my jeans down, and slides my panties to one side, and gives me his fingers.

I expect him to go straight for my clit, rubbing it furiously the way Steven used to. Desperate to get me off so he could take his turn. Overstimulating me, not listening to my body or what I wanted. Forcing me to fake it just so it's over.

Instead, he stares at me, studies my face, as he drags one torturous finger over my soaking wet slit. He strokes me, my inner thighs, my folds, my entrance. He applies pressure, then takes it away. He makes circles, and lines, and never takes his gaze from mine.

My nipples stiffen and strain against the inside of my bra. I desperately want him to tug down my shirt and expose my breasts. I want him to take one in his mouth and suck.

As the thought enters my head, he narrows his eyes.

"What do you want?" he asks in a timbre that makes my knees shake.

I shake my head. "Just keep doing that." I look down at his hand. His fingers have found my clit and they're making feather-light circles around it. Not touching it. Not yet.

"What else?" he asks.

When I don't reply, he uses his other hand to hold my jaw, so my mouth opens. Then he spits into my mouth.

The gesture shocks me. Makes me feel disgustingly dirty and unbelievably turned on at the same time. I grip the dresser harder. He is still holding my mouth open, and he is now pinching my clit. Hard.

I wince as pain and pleasure collide in my core.

"What do you want?" He repeats the question, loosening his grip on my chin so I can speak.

"I want your mouth…"

"What do you want me to do with my mouth, Luna?"

My entire body feels hot and cold all over. Why is this so difficult? It's like my voice is trapped in my ribcage, straining against my chest. "I want you to play with my nipples."

He growls as I speak, like he's incredibly turned on by hearing me say the words. The look on his face gives me the confidence to continue.

"I want you to use your mouth, and your tongue. Suck. Hard."

He lets go of my chin, then nods for me to take my top off.

I pull it over my head and toss it onto the armchair next to the dresser.

Lucien smiles. It makes his square, chiseled jaw twitch and his eyes glimmer with that little freckle of scarlet I saw before.

He nods approvingly, then unclasps my bra, and lifts it to his face.

He inhales the scent of it, and I'm both a little weirded out and incredibly turned on at the same time.

He drops the bra then lowers his mouth to my left breast. As he seals his lips over my nipple, and caresses it with his tongue, his fingers start to move again. Not pinching now, but stroking. Gentle, slow circles.

He mirrors the movement with his tongue on my nipple.

"I asked you to suck…" The words pass my lips before I have the chance to stop them, and I'm shocked at myself. A look of panic crosses my face. My stomach clenches, and my heartbeat quickens.

But Lucien simply looks up at me, meets my gaze, and does as he's told. He sucks, and when I nod, he sucks harder.

The tension between my legs is building. My arms are straining from bracing my weight, still supporting me by holding onto the dresser.

"I need to hold onto you." I stand up a little straighter and flex my fingers.

The distraction of pain is always guaranteed to stop an orgasm in its tracks.

Lucien grabs my arms and loops them around his neck, then wraps his arm around my waist. "I've got you," he growls. "You can come for me now, Luna."

I'm about to tell him that's unlikely to happen when he returns his mouth to my breasts. His tongue moves faster this time, sucking and flicking at the same time.

His fingers speed up too. Not too hard, but fast.

They move to my entrance, and two of them thrust inside me.

Then back to my clit.

I have no idea how he's moving so fast, and how he seems to know my body better than I do already.

I cry out, every muscle coiling and straining.

I cling onto him. My knees shake, my toes curl in my shoes.

I feel like I'm going to collapse onto the floor, but he holds me tight and says, again and again, "I've got you. I've got you."

When my orgasm finally explodes, I dig my nails into his back, gripping him tightly, breathing hard, pressed against his chest.

He lifts his head from my breasts and takes his hand from between my legs. Then he tilts my chin and kisses me.

Our lips meet, soft and searching. For a long time, we explore each other. Standing there, kissing. When we stop, he stands back and folds his arms, watching me. Still shaking, I pull up my jeans. I feel suddenly, completely exposed. I reach for my bra and my top, but he grabs them before I do then snatches up my cardigan too.

His tenderness has disappeared, and there is frustration in his eyes now.

"You'll have these back when you start believing I brought you here for your safety."

He curls his fist around my clothes. Then turns and strides out of the room, locking the door behind him.

CHAPTER 11
LUCIEN

I stand with my back to the closed bedroom door and feel my fingernails dig into my palm as I clasp her clothes tightly in my fist.

My cock is harder than it has been in months. Racing through my veins is a primal, animalistic urge to rip that door from its hinges, and go back into her room, and devour her. I want to hear her whimper again; except this time, I want to watch her eyes widen as I thrust deep inside her.

I want to see her lips quiver, hear my name on her tongue. I want her voice, the one she keeps buried inside, to tell me exactly how hard she wants it. Because even though she *looks* the picture of innocence, there's something fluttering beneath the surface of her gaze that tells me she wants to be ruined.

She wants it hard, and fast, and sweaty, and dirty.

And somehow, hearing those filthy things from her, on her honey-sweet tongue, makes them even more torturous.

Unfastening my belt, I wrap my hand around my cock and

start to stroke it. I want release. But then I stop because I don't want it like this; I want it with her.

Inside her.

I want to come while I watch her come.

I turn around and press my palm against her door. A dog-like growl parts my lips and I feel them curl on top of my fangs.

She tasted good. Her blood is sweet and thick, but it isn't the most powerful I've ever tasted, which surprises me.

It has made me horny as fuck. But it hasn't made me supercharged or stronger or any of the things I'd expect if I'm right about who she is. *What* she is.

Refastening my belt, I stride away from her, trying not to think about her half-naked body curled up in *my* bed in *my* house, pulling the blankets up to cover her perfectly full breasts and her rose red nipples.

Fuck, those nipples.

And the way her voice deepened when she told me to suck them.

I am still hard as hell by the time I reach my study. Immediately, I take my phone from the top drawer and text Kim. *Get back here, now. I have another job for you.*

He doesn't reply, but I know he'll do as I say.

He hates me, but he needs me.

I need him too. A human who can do things in daylight that I can't.

It is an arrangement that works, even though both of us wish we didn't need it to.

While I wait for him, I go to the kennels and release the dogs. I let them sniff Luna's shirt – I keep her bra in my pocket – then open the door to the garden and watch as they race in the direction of her bedroom and position themselves beneath the broken window.

If she tries to move the painting and escape again, they will stop her. There is no way she'll escape me. Not now.

Slamming the door shut, listening to the dogs barking, I scratch my forearms. They still itch from the sunlight, and my cock is still hard as fuck for Luna.

Back in the study, I sit down at my desk. Instinctively, even though she's here and not there, I navigate to the security cameras for the bookshop.

Light streams in through the window. Kim did a good job of cleaning up; everything looks completely normal. As if Luna's going to appear at any moment and open up.

I'm still staring at it when Kim arrives. He knocks but enters at the same time and stands in the doorway with an expression on his face I can't quite read.

"Well?"

He clocks the camera feed of the bookshop and nods at it. "Were you watching me the whole time, or…?"

"I was not watching you. I had more important things to do."

Kim flops down into the armchair opposite my desk, and folds one leg over the other. He's holding a reusable take out coffee cup with a black silicon lid. The combination of the coffee and the silicon assaults my nose; two smells I can't stand.

Ignoring the look of displeasure on my face, but clearly understanding it has something to do with the coffee, Kim takes a leisurely sip and fixes his gaze on mine.

"What did you find at the bookshop?"

"Nothing." Kim shrugs. "It felt creepy as fuck in there. A lot of demonic energy floating about. But you did murder three vampires there, so…"

"Four," I mutter.

"Right. Four. Sorry, I lost count of the body parts."

"Did you retrieve the box?"

"No box."

I frown at him, and he holds up his palm as if he knows I think he's lying. "There was no box, Lucien. Lots of blood. Lots of gore. Lots of powerful juju in the air, but no box and no dancing shadows."

"That doesn't mean I'm wrong."

"No, it doesn't."

"Can you be serious for a moment and tell me what you really think?"

"You care what I think?"

"You hunt demons for a living, boy. You have hunter blood. So, yes, I care what you think about the demonic energy in my shop."

"Your shop?" Kim's mouth drops open a little. "I *knew* it... you own that place?"

I ignore the question.

Kim sighs and leans forward onto his knees. "Okay. Seriously? It's strong. That's all I can tell you. Not bad, not dark, not good, not light. Just *strong*. But it's just an essence. Like whatever the powerful thing was is gone now."

"I see." I glance back at the screen and steeple my fingers together.

"You said you had another job for me?" Kim sits back in his chair.

"I need you to board up a window." I reply absentmindedly, drumming my fingernails on the desk.

"Board up a window?" Kim uncrosses his legs and shakes his head, so his curls move across his eyes. When he swipes them away, he stands up and moves toward the door.

"I'm not a fucking handyman," he says. He's wearing a white shirt and slacks. He still looks like someone who works a respectable office job. An accountant or someone who works in insurance. But his *aura* is different these days. Since he decided to embrace his destiny as a demon hunter, he's carried himself differently. He's talked to me differently.

I respect him for it.

But I don't like it.

"We have an agreement," I remind him.

Kim braces a hand on the door frame. His back stiffens as he holds his breath in his chest then sighs. When he turns to face me, he leans against the wall and crosses his arms in front of his stomach. "Fine," he says. "Fix a window. Why and where?"

"In Luna's room. Because she tried to escape."

His expression changes. His forehead creases and there's a flicker of irritation, maybe even anger, in his eyes. "What did you do to her? You said you brought her here to *protect* her while we try to figure out—"

"I didn't do anything to her." My lips twitch as the image of her shaking and orgasming onto my hand dances through my mind. "Not before the escape, at least. She made that decision completely unprompted by anything I'd done."

Kim's jaw twitches. "I don't like this, Lucien. If the girl wants to leave—"

Rage blooms in my gut. I stand up and slam my fists on the desk. I feel my eyes flash red, and I feel her blood – the tiny amount I licked from her hand – flutter in my throat. "If she leaves, she could die!" I shout so loudly the lights rattle and the walls seem to creak.

"We have no proof of that, Lucien. The vampires who attacked her were there because of the box." Kim is speaking calmly and firmly, unrattled by my display of anger.

I leave the desk and start pacing the room. I want to break something. I flex my fingers, clench my fists, then pick up the decanter of whiskey on the sideboard and throw it at the wall. It shatters, stains the wallpaper, and the scent of the alcohol fills the air.

"They were there because of *her*!"

Raising his hands as if he's surrendering, Kim says, "All right, okay, I'll fix the window. But you need to promise you won't hurt her."

I swallow hard, throat twitching at the thought of the deep, scarlet liquid that dripped down her arm when she cut herself. "She is already hurt. She cut herself when she broke the window. See to that, too." I hesitate then meet his eyes. "While you're with her…"

Kim nods and rolls his eyes slightly. "I'll see if I can get a read on her. If I sense the same energy."

"Good." I roll my tongue over my teeth then reach into my pocket and take out the key to Luna's room. "Give this back when you're done."

He looks at the key, then at me, and sighs a little. "Fine. Where are your tools?"

I frown at him. "Tools?"

"Hammer? Nails?"

I wave a dismissive hand. "Basement somewhere."

"And a first aid kit?"

"You think I own a *first aid* kit? I'm a vampire, Kim. I heal on my own."

Kim slurps the last of his coffee. The noise grates at my temples. "You really need to employ some more people. Big scary mafia guy like you, shouldn't you have a house full of staff to do this shit?"

I step toward him, foot crunching on the broken decanter. "I tried that. It didn't work out," I mutter through gritted teeth. "I keep my inner circle close these days."

"If you say so." Kim shakes his head, disappearing through the door and closing it behind him.

He's part way down the corridor when I hear him say, "Fucking vamps. Crazy mother fuckers."

I return to my desk and re-open the bookshop feed, then take the flask of blood from the drawer. Taking a long swig, holding it in my mouth for a second to savor the taste, I flick to the previous recordings from the shop and find the one that shows Luna receiving the box.

I press play and sit back.

"Yeah," I mutter as I watch her opening the box and peering inside, shadows flickering. "We are crazy mother fuckers."

CHAPTER 12
LUNA

Despite Lucien slamming the painting back over the window, it is freezing in here. Fingers of icy cold air sneak in through the gaps between the back of the picture frame and the open window, and they trail over my exposed skin making me shiver.

I rub my arms and reach for the blanket at the foot of the bed. I wrap it around myself, but it still doesn't feel like enough.

And I'm still breathless and shaky from the orgasm he wrung from my trembling body.

I have never come like that before. Steven *never* made me feel like that. In fact, for the last three years the only orgasms I've had have been the sad, quiet, hurried ones I've had in the shower or in bed at night when he was out at the pub with his friends, and I dared to remember what it was like to feel turned on.

The way Lucien touched me... it was as if he already knew me. The way he gave me a voice and made me ask for what I wanted... no one has ever done that for me before. I shocked myself, and I aroused him. I could feel it in the way his cock stiffened against me when he pressed up close, and I could see it in his eyes.

He *wanted* me. And in those moments, even though I knew he could still hurt me if he wanted to, I felt safe.

I believed what he said about protecting me.

But then he ruined it by stalking out of here, taking my clothes with him, and locking me back inside.

My head is spinning. The buzz of arousal is mixing with fear and confusion, and I can't distinguish any one emotion from another. It's like they are swirling together in one big hazy vortex of fuckery that I don't know what to do with.

I'm curling into the armchair, pulling my knees up to my chest, ready to have a cry because it's the only thing I can think of that might release these feelings when I hear the key in the door.

I stand up and, fuck knows why, but a sudden burst of bravery makes me toss the blanket to the floor and put my hands on my hips. "Did you bring my clothes back? Or are you here to ask me more questions? Because forget sucking my nipples, what I want right now is to get out of this godforsaken hell hole of a—"

I stop mid-speech when I realize the man backing into the room, carrying what looks like a large sheet of MDF and a hammer, is *not* Lucien Thornfield.

Whoever the fuck he is, he sets the MDF down by the wall, closes the door, locks it again, slips the key into his pocket then turns to look at me,

I'm still standing with my hands on my hips, brazenly, as if I don't care that I'm half naked.

He raises his eyebrows. They're light brown, and thick, but half obscured by a pair of round tortoiseshell glasses. Brushing his curly hair from his face, he rolls up his white shirt sleeves and very deliberately looks away from me.

"I'm afraid I don't have your clothes, I don't have any questions for you right now, and I'm not adverse to sucking your nipples but I feel like we should at least exchange names first. Unless you're asking to suck mine, in which case..." He pauses, scratching his chin. "No, I still think we should introduce ourselves first. Maybe get a drink. Or dinner."

I grab the blanket, cheeks flaming beetroot red, and wrap it around myself like a towel, covering my breasts, wishing I had my bra on because they do *not* defy the laws of gravity and are nowhere near as pert as they should be.

"I'm so sorry. I thought you were..."

The man glances at me, realizes I'm covered, then points at the painting. "Window behind there?" he asks.

I nod, sinking back into the chair.

He takes the painting down and whistles, shaking his head. "You broke the glass?" he asks.

I nod, and gesture to the candlestick which is still on the floor nearby.

"Oh shit, nearly forgot..." He strides over to me and grabs my hand.

The sudden contact makes me flinch, but when I look up and meet his eyes, a sense of warmth settles in my stomach instead.

"Thornfield told me to fix your hand up."

I raise a skeptical eyebrow.

"True story," the man says, holding up a finger. "Bathroom in here?" He gestures to a door opposite the bed.

I nod; I checked it out as soon as he locked me in here. But there was nothing useful. Just a plain white room with a toilet, a sink, a shower and – weirdly – the exact shampoo I've used for about the last five years.

The man disappears inside and comes back with a damp towel. He kneels in front of me and holds my wrist, then cleans the cut on my palm. His touch is slow and gentle, and as he wipes the blood from my skin there is no flicker of blood lust or hunger in his eyes.

"You're not a vampire?" I ask him.

He shakes his head, then reaches into his pocket and takes out a tube of antiseptic cream. He dabs it on gently, then pulls out a plaster. It has cartoon cats on it. I chuckle as he presses it to my skin.

"I was with my nieces and nephews at the weekend. Sophia cut her knee. Thankfully, still had these in my car because Thornfield has fuck all in the way of human first-aid around here."

"I guess he brings his humans here to eat them not heal them," I reply, tilting my head to study the man's square jaw and grey-brown eyes.

He laughs and stands up. "Don't worry. He won't be eating you," he says. Something flits across his face, but he bites the corner of his lip as if he's stopping himself from saying it. Like a schoolboy who wants to shout a rude joke in class. He clears his throat. "He doesn't feed from humans these days. Not often, anyway."

He returns to the window and uses his elbow to brush all the remaining shards of glass free.

Below, the dogs that Thornfield sent to bark below my window start making noise.

"I'm Kim, by the way." He strides back to the discarded sheet of MDF then takes it to the window.

"Luna," I reply, twisting so I can watch as he takes nails from his pocket and starts to hammer the MDF into place. "You work for Lucien?"

Kim pauses, considering his words carefully. "You could say that."

"What exactly does he do?" I ask, curiosity getting the better of me. From when he visited the bookshop, I know he works for the university, but I also know you don't get to be the owner of a huge mansion, and have staff at your beck and call, on a university professor's salary.

Kim glances at me over his shoulder and bites the inside of his cheek as if he's trying to decide how to answer me. "I suppose the best way to phrase it is…" He frowns, searching for the right words. "The thing is, Thornfield… he's not just a vampire. He's essentially the supernatural mafia boss of Cambridge."

My eyes widen but then I laugh a little. "Mafia?"

Kim raises his eyebrows. "Oh yeah. He runs the Fermented Human Blood trade in the city. FHB."

"I've heard of it."

"Then you know it's a big deal. Thornfield controls who sells it, who buys it, everything. He's got his fingers in a lot of pies, and let's just say he's not someone you want to cross."

I absorb this information, feeling a mix of shock and… something else. Fear? Excitement? "And you're okay working for someone like that?"

Kim shrugs. "Like I said, it's complicated. But Thornfield… he keeps things in check. Without him, it'd be chaos."

I watch as Kim finishes hammering the MDF into place over the broken window.

With the daylight gone again, my chest tightens; I've always hated the dark.

"Does he keep you locked up here, too?" I adjust my glasses on the bridge of my nose. "Or does he pay you for odd jobs?"

Kim laughs and, instead of hanging the picture back up, props it in front of the wardrobe. "No. We're… colleagues." He perches on the end of the bed and crosses his legs at the ankles. He sits quietly for a moment, studying me with a mixture of curiosity and concern.

I shift in my chair, wincing as a sharp pain shoots through my lower back. The constant ache I've been trying to ignore since arriving here is steadily growing worse, and I can feel my muscles tensing in response.

"Are you all right?" Kim asks gently.

I force a smile; the kind I'm used to giving people a hundred times a day. The one that perfectly masks how I'm really feeling. "Fine. Apart from being kidnapped and held hostage."

"I'm not sure you're a hostage," Kim says. There's something about him that puts me at ease, despite the bizarre situation. Maybe it's his calm demeanor or the way he fixed my hand without hesitation. Whatever it is, I find myself wanting to trust him, even though I know I shouldn't trust anyone in this place.

"Kim," I start, trying to keep my voice steady, "why does Lucien think I need protecting? What's really going on here?"

He looks away, his jaw tightening slightly.

"Please. Thornfield won't talk to me, and I can't just sit here alone with my thoughts. It will drive me crazy."

Kim sighs a little then adjusts his glasses on his nose. "Because of what happened at the bookshop. The vampires who attacked you. He thinks they might return."

I lean forward, ignoring the twinge in my muscles. There is more to it than that. I know there is. But neither of them wants to tell me the truth. "One of the vampires mentioned something about a queen. What did they mean?"

Kim runs a hand through his curly hair. The gesture is oddly endearing, making him seem more approachable. It's a stark contrast to Lucien's gothic, otherworldly presence.

"There used to be a vampire queen named Zephyra," he explains. "She ran the Fermented Human Blood trade in Cambridge. Lucien had an arrangement with her - she could deal FHB if she kept the vampire population under control. And gave him a healthy share of her profits."

As he speaks, I notice the way his shoulders tense, as if the memory itself is uncomfortable. I wonder how deeply he's involved in this world of vampires and blood trades.

"What happened?" I ask, rubbing my temples to ease the growing tension headache. The pain is spreading, creeping up from my lower back to my shoulders, making it hard to concentrate.

"She double-crossed him. Lucien had to... end her reign." Kim's voice is cautious, measured. He's clearly choosing his words carefully, and I can't help but wonder what he's not telling me.

A chill runs down my spine as I remember the vampire's words. "They said Lucien ate her heart. Is that true?"

"He did. And... so did I."

I frown at him for a moment then feel myself recoil slightly, shock coursing through me. The pain momentarily forgotten as I try to process the image forming in my mind. "But you're human. Why would you...?"

Kim stands abruptly, moving towards the door. His sudden movement makes me flinch, and I hate myself for it. He doesn't seem like a threat, but after everything that's happened, I can't help but be on edge.

"I'm human, yes, but I'm also a demon hunter. I have hunter blood," he explains, his voice tight. "It's a long story."

"I have time," I tell him, trying to smile.

He doesn't smile back. "I was struggling to accept my identity. Eating the heart seemed symbolic. A good idea at the time."

As he reaches for the doorknob, I call out, ignoring the stabbing pain in my joints as I stand up, blanket wrapped tightly around me. "Wait! I have a favor to ask."

He pauses, turning back to me with a softness in his eyes that wasn't there before. It is so different from the way Lucien looks at me.

I take a deep breath, trying to push past the discomfort. My whole body feels like it's on fire now, each movement sending waves of pain through me. "Could you ask Lucien if he can get my pills from the bookshop? I'm in a lot of pain, and I really need them."

Kim's expression softens further. He nods, "I'll ask him. No promises, but I'll try." He hesitates for a moment, then asks, "Are you going to try to escape again?"

The question catches me off guard. I look up at him, searching his face for any sign of what he thinks I should do. "Do you think I should?"

Kim looks thoughtful, his brow furrowing slightly. After a moment, he replies, "On the whole I'd say, right now, you're safer here than anywhere else." He meets my eyes, his gaze steady and sincere. "But if that changes, I promise I will tell you."

The weight of his words settles over me. I nod slowly, processing what he's said. There's something reassuring about his promise, even though I barely know him.

As he leaves, locking the door behind him, I curl up in the chair, hugging my knees to my chest. The pain is getting worse. Even if I wanted to escape, the adrenaline and exertion of my first attempt has rendered me next to useless.

I stand and cross over to the bed. I lie down, but I am no more comfortable here than I was in the chair.

Staring at the drapes that box in the four-poster bed, I try to focus on my breathing and not the way my body feels.

I feel suddenly lonely, and the weight of being completely trapped presses down on my fragile chest.

I close my eyes and picture the kindness in Kim's eyes.

I can't help but compare him to Lucien. Where Lucien is all intensity and danger, Kim seems... normal. Almost reassuringly so. But then I remember what he said about eating a vampire queen's heart, and being a demon hunter, and I shudder. Maybe there are no normal people in this world I've fallen into.

I turn onto my side and prop a pillow between my legs – a trick a physiotherapist showed me once to help ease the ache in my lower body.

It doesn't help much.

The pain is becoming unbearable now. And without my medication, I know it will only get worse.

I try using the techniques I've learned over the years to manage the pain – breathwork, meditation, tapping – but it's hard to concentrate. My mind keeps wandering back to the events at the bookshop, to Lucien's intense gaze, to Kim's gentle hands as he bandaged my cut.

I wonder if Kim will really ask Lucien about my meds or if he was just saying that to placate me. And even if he does ask, will Lucien care?

As another wave of pain washes over me, I close my eyes tightly. I'm trapped in this room, in this mansion, in this body that feels like it's betraying me.

I have no idea how I'm going to get out of any of it. Or if i'll have a job to return to when I do because, surely, if I fail to turn up to work for more than twenty-four-hours my boss will fire me.

But Kim's words echo in my mind – I'm safer here.

For now.

CHAPTER 13

KIM

I close the door behind me, and linger for a moment longer than necessary. The image of Luna, half-naked and vulnerable, is seared into my brain. Fuck. Seeing her like that, it took everything I had not to stare.

She looks so much like Sarah it's uncanny. The same curves, the same soft skin, even the way she tilts her head when she's thinking. It's like seeing a ghost, except this ghost is very much alive and currently locked in a vampire's spare room.

I start walking down the hallway, my mind racing. I tried to play it cool, act like I wasn't affected by the fact she was missing half her clothes. But who am I kidding? She's stunning. The kind of beautiful that makes you forget how to breathe for a second and sends heat straight to your cock.

Running a hand through my hair, I try to shake off the memories of Sarah that are threatening to overwhelm me. It's not fair to Luna to compare her to my dead wife. And it's not fair to Sarah, either.

Luna is her own person with her own story. A story that's

currently tangled up with vampires, demon hunters, and god knows what else. And she's beautiful in her own right. Not just because she reminds me of the only woman I ever loved.

As I draw further away from her, her question echoes in my mind.

She asked if she should try to escape, and I told her to stay.

Was that the right thing to say?

The urge to protect her hits me like a punch to the gut. It's irrational and sudden, but undeniable.

But protect her from what, exactly? Lucien seems genuinely concerned for her safety, even if his methods are questionable. The vampire attack at the bookshop was real enough. But then there's the shadow magick we saw on the security footage. If she really does have that kind of power, she might need protection from herself. Or from Lucien... because I have no idea what he wants with her if she turns out to be who he thinks she is.

Maybe it's neither of those things.

Maybe I just want to protect her from the pain she's in. The way she winced when she moved, the tightness around her eyes — it's clear she's suffering.

Well, fuck that.

I might not be able to set her free, but I don't have to watch her suffer.

I stop in my tracks, decision made. I'm not going to ask Lucien about getting her pills. I'm just going to do it. He can throw a fit later if he wants, but I'm not leaving Luna in pain when I can do something about it.

This is probably a terrible idea. Lucien's not exactly known for his forgiving nature, especially when it comes to people going behind his back. But the thought of her curled up in that chair, hurting and alone, makes my chest ache in a way I haven't felt in a long time.

Before leaving, I drop back into Lucien's office, return the key to Luna's room, tell him she's fine, and that I didn't sense anything weird about her energy – which is true, by the way. Then I make up some bullshit about going to ask questions in town, and head out.

As I slide into the driver's seat of my beat-up Volvo, I can't help laughing at the absurdity of it all.

I'm defying a powerful vampire to fetch medication for a woman I barely know, all because she reminds me of my dead wife.

Sarah would've found this hilarious. She always said I had a hero complex.

∼

THE BOOKSHOP IS EERILY quiet when I arrive, and once again I can't shake the feeling that I'm being watched.

Paranoia or hunter instinct?

These days, it's hard to tell the difference.

I use the spare key Lucien gave me earlier and slip inside. The smell of old books and lingering vampire guts hits me immediately.

Despite my thorough clean-up job, there's still an undercurrent of supernatural energy that makes my skin prickle.

Luna's medication isn't hard to find. It's right there in the desk drawer, a plain white box with her name printed on it. As I pick it up, I catch sight of her address on the label.

A plan forms in my mind before I can talk myself out of it.

"In for a penny, in for a pound," I mutter, pocketing the pills and heading back to my car.

It doesn't take long to cross the city. Luna's house is a small, quaint place on a quiet street. It looks so normal, so untouched by the chaos of the past twenty-four-hours, that it's almost jarring. I use my lock-picking skills – a questionable but useful talent for a demon hunter – to let myself in.

The moment I step inside, I know something's wrong. The air is thick with an oppressive energy that makes my hunter instincts scream. The living room is a mess – furniture overturned, books scattered across the floor, picture frames smashed.

This isn't just a burglary. This is a vampire's handiwork. I can sense it.

I draw my blade. My footsteps are silent on the wooden floors as I navigate the chaos.

The kitchen is similarly ransacked, drawers pulled out and contents strewn about. But it's not just random destruction – there's a method to this madness. Whoever caused it was looking for something.

As I approach the bedroom, the vampiric energy intensifies. It's like walking through syrup, each step requiring more effort than the last. My heart pounds in my chest, blood rushing in my ears.

I used to hate this sensation. Now, I thrive on it.

I pause at the closed bedroom door, listening. There's no sound from within but that doesn't mean much with vampires. I take a deep breath, steeling myself, then slowly turn the knob.

The door creaks open, revealing Luna's bedroom bathed in shadows. The curtains are drawn, blocking out the sun. In the dim light, I can make out the same destruction as in the rest of the house – clothes thrown about, drawers emptied.

And there, sprawled across Luna's bed, is a vampire.

He's young or, at least, he was when he was turned. Couldn't be more than twenty.

I grip my blade tighter, weighing my options. I could end him now, quickly and quietly. But a dead vampire can't answer questions. And I want to know what the fuck he was looking for.

As I stand there, trying to decide whether to stake it or torture it, the vampire's eyes snap open. They lock onto mine, confusion quickly morphing into hunger.

"Well," he says, sitting up with inhuman speed, "this is unexpected."

I raise my blade. It is silver, and sharp enough to end him with one stab to the heart. "Who sent you here?"

He grins, revealing gleaming fangs. "Wouldn't you like to know, hunter?"

How do they *always* know I'm a hunter?

And then he lunges.

His speed is impressive, but I'm ready for him. I sidestep him, bringing my blade up in a swift arc. It catches him across the chest, drawing a hiss of pain and anger as his skin bubbles from contact with the silver.

We dance around the room. He's strong but sloppy. I use that to my advantage, letting him wear himself out with wild swings and lunges.

Finally, I see my opening. As he charges me again, I drop low and sweep his legs out from under him. He crashes to the floor, and before he can recover, I'm on him, pinning him down with my blade at his throat.

"Let's try this again," I growl, reaching out with my free hand to yank the curtains open. Sunlight floods the room, and the vampire screams as his exposed skin begins to smoke and blister.

I shift my position, allowing a beam of sunlight to fall directly on his face. He writhes in agony, trying to turn away, but I hold him still.

"What were you looking for?"

He doesn't answer, just writhes beneath me.

"Who sent you?" I demand, easing the sunlight off his face momentarily.

He pants, his eyes wild. "He will destroy you... all of you..."

"Who?" I press the blade harder against his throat. "Who sent you?"

Before he can answer, there's a blur of movement behind me. I whirl around, blade at the ready, but I'm not fast enough.

Another vampire, this one older and far more skilled, materializes in the room. Before I can react, he's driven a wooden stake through the heart of the vampire I was interrogating.

The young vampire crumbles to dust beneath me, and I leap to my feet. But the older vampire doesn't attack. Instead, he locks eyes with me.

"You'll get no answers here, hunter," he says, his voice gravelly and resigned.

And then he plunges the stake into his own heart.

In an instant, he too is nothing but a pile of ash on Luna's bedroom floor.

I stand there, blade still raised, heart pounding. Whatever's going on here, Luna is caught right in the middle of it.

I pinch the bridge of my nose. I still don't know if I can trust that Thornfield wants to keep her safe but I have no choice; I need to tell him what I know because *without* him, she is definitely in danger.

CHAPTER 14
LUNA

I am still freezing cold, and the sun is setting, which means it's going to get even colder in here.

I can't see any radiators.

There's a fireplace, but the fire isn't lit.

Taking my third scalding hot shower of the day, I resist the urge to wash my hair because leaving it to dry damp on my bare skin would be unbearable.

I stand under the water for a long time.

The sting of heat distracts me from the ache in my body.

Ache isn't really the right word; it's more like my nerves are on fire, sending electric shocks through my muscles and bones.

Sometimes it's a dull, persistent throb. As if someone's beating a drum inside my body. Other times, it's sharp and stabbing like tiny shards of glass are embedded in my joints, grinding with every movement.

The pain migrates, never staying in one place for long. One moment it's concentrated in my lower back, a deep, gnawing ache that makes standing straight feel impossible. The next, it's shooting down my legs, making them feel heavy and weak, like they might give out at any second.

My skin feels hypersensitive, like it's been rubbed raw. Even the soft touch of my clothes can feel abrasive, sending ripples of discomfort across my body. There's a constant underlying tension, as if my muscles are always braced for impact, never truly relaxed.

And the fatigue that comes with it is just as overwhelming. It's not just tiredness – it's a bone-deep exhaustion that makes even the simplest tasks feel monumental. My brain feels foggy, thoughts slipping away before I can fully grasp them.

But the hardest thing about it is the unpredictability of it all. Some days, the pain is a quiet whisper in the background. Other days, even *with* my meds, it's a roaring monster that consumes everything, making it hard to focus on anything else.

As I finally step out of the shower, wrapping myself in a towel, I brace for the wave of pain that I know will come with the change in temperature and movement. It's always there, waiting, a constant companion I never asked for and can't seem to shake.

I hate it.

I hate that it is part of me, and that I can't escape it.

I hate that there is no answer, no fix, no solution.

I hate that I look normal. That no one can see the way I feel.

I should be black and blue, swollen, covered in bruises, limbs jutting out at strange broken angles. I shouldn't smile. I shouldn't laugh. I should stop trying to pretend I'm okay, but I'm terrified that if I give in and allow myself to admit that I'm not, I'll be handing *it* the power.

The pain will consume me.

Ignoring it. Drowning it out. Smiling wider, laughing louder, being so *okay* that no one will ever guess... that is how I win.

I take a deep breath, allowing the air to swell in my chest.

The true danger is that with pain comes darkness. The kind that settles in the between my bones and feels heavy. All consuming.

The undulating, undeniable need to take control of something swarms beneath my skin.

I glance toward the bathroom and think about the razor in the shower. My fingers go to my leg. I lift up the towel and look down at the silvery scars on my thigh.

I'd like to say it has been a long time since I hurt myself.

It has not.

Just before Steven disappeared, I gave in to the urges that used to consume me daily and are now confined to my darkest most desperate days.

But I can't do that here, can I?

He'd smell the blood.

He'd know, and what if this time he couldn't control himself?

I let out a frustrated sigh and lean forward, scraping my fingers through my hair.

When I stand, I pull my underwear and my jeans back on, then wrap the blanket around my chest. I hang the towel on the hook behind the bathroom door and study my reflection in the mirror, trying not to make eye contact with the razor by the sink.

Through the condensation, my skin looks smoother and more palatable than usual.

I wipe some of the condensation away with the corner of the blanket, revealing a clearer view of myself. My blonde curls are a mess, frizzy and untamed without product to keep them in check. I've always had a love-hate relationship with my hair — it's unique, but often unruly.

Right now, it looks like a flock of birds have been nesting in it.

I reach for my glasses and as soon as I lift them to my face, they fog up slightly. My blue eyes peer back at me through the mist. I've never considered my eyes particularly striking, but they're probably the feature I like the most. Especially if I use a little makeup.

I'm not a heavy makeup kind of person, but mascara and eyeliner are my go-to.

Right now, the remnants of yesterday's makeup are smudged beneath my eyes. I push my glasses on top of my head and dampen some tissue paper to try and remove the stains on my face.

It doesn't work. The smudges just get bigger.

I sigh and brush my fingers over my flushed cheeks. Still pink from the heat of the shower.

My skin is usually pale, with a smattering of freckles across my nose and cheeks. No amount of sun seems to give me a tan, just more freckles. But I've learned to accept them as part of my look.

Beneath the makeup, I notice the dark circles under my eyes, a testament to the lack of sleep over the past twenty-four hours.

I stand up straighter and flex my fingers at my sides.

My arms ache.

I flex them, too. As if stretching might help.

As I move, the blanket slips a bit, and I catch a glimpse of my curves. I'm not skinny, never have been. I have big hips, a big bum, and a rounded stomach, definitely more padding than society typically deems ideal.

Definitely more than Steven deemed appropriate.

Sighing, I adjust the blanket and turn away from the mirror. I hate that he is still in my head even though he's gone.

I close my eyes for a moment and recall the memory of the video Lucien showed me. I think about Steven's face, and his piss-stained pants, and the pathetic mumbled apology that became more and more desperate as he tried to save his own life.

Frustration blooms in my gut.

For the first time, I feel angry that he is gone. Not because I miss him but because I should have been the one to stand up to him and make him apologize.

I should have been brave enough. I should have stood over him and made him grovel at my feet.

"Luna?" Lucien's voice tugs me back into the room.

I step out of the bathroom and find him standing in front of me holding a wooden tray. On top of it is a steaming bowl of what looks like pasta, a glass of water, and... my pills.

My eyes widen.

"Kim tells me you asked him to fetch these for you." He sets the tray down on the bed and picks up the pill packet.

I move closer, slowly, half expecting him to tease me with them the way Steven would have. Hold them out of reach. Taunt me for needing them.

Instead, he presses them into my palm and says, "You should have asked me." He curls his fingers over mine. The contact sends a shiver through me.

"I didn't think you'd let me have them," I say bluntly, still fuzzy from the feeling of his hand on mine.

Lucien's brow creases into a displeased frown. "I want you to be safe. And I would *never* want you to be in pain."

I have no idea why, but as he stares at me, I believe what he's saying. His words land like kisses on my skin. Tingling heat settles between my legs.

"I will do anything I can to prevent you from suffering, Luna." He moves his hand to my wrist and tugs me closer. His other hand is on my waist. It slips beneath the blanket and his fingertips brush my stomach.

Why does he love that part of me so much?

I don't understand it.

He leans closer. My lips part in anticipation of his kiss, but then he jerks away from me and thrusts a glass of water into my free hand. "Take your pills. I want you to feel better."

I stare at the packet, then at the glass of water.

"I'll take them if you tell me why I'm here." I mutter the words without looking at him. When he doesn't respond, and I feel his body stiffen, I know I have got to him.

This is how I take back control.

"You can't bear to see me suffer. You will do *anything* to prevent it." I push back my shoulders and tilt my chin.

For some reason, I feel more able to challenge this vampire than I felt able to challenge Steven.

"So, then, Lucien... tell me why you are keeping me here. The real reason."

"You were attacked. I killed your assailants. More will come." His eyes are shimmering with frustration. "You have your answer, now take the pills."

"That's not the real answer." I put my hands on my hips. I want to sit down. And I want to take the pills. But right now, this is all I have... this is the only thing I can control.

"Why do you think that?"

"I can see it in your face. There is something you're not telling me. And it doesn't add up. Why would more vampires come for me? I'm of no interest to them."

The muscles in Lucien's shoulders twitch. He is biting down on his anger. I can see him quite literally grinding his teeth as he struggles to keep it in check. His eyes flash with a mixture of frustration and something else – concern, perhaps? He turns abruptly, striding towards the door.

"There are clothes on the bed," he says, his voice tight with restrained emotion. "Kim brought them from your house." His hand rests on the doorknob. "But until you take those pills, you'll live like I do. In utter darkness."

Before I can respond, he's out of the door. I hear the lock click into place and, suddenly, all the lights in the room go out. The darkness is immediate and complete, so thick it feels like a physical presence pressing against my skin.

Panic rises in my chest, a suffocating wave that threatens to overwhelm me. I've always hated the dark, found it oppressive and terrifying. The blackness seems to amplify every sound, every sensation. My breath comes in short, sharp gasps.

My father used to do this.

Leave me in the dark.

Alone.

I stumble forward, arms outstretched, trying to find my bearings. My hip collides painfully with what must be the edge of the bed. I swear under my breath, fighting the urge to call out for Lucien, to beg him to turn the lights back on.

But I can't give in. Not yet.

I'm still holding the pill packet, and for a moment, I'm tempted. The pain is still there, a constant throb that seems to intensify in the darkness. But I resist.

I need answers. Real ones. And if this is what it takes to get them, then so be it.

If he really can't stand to see me in pain, then surely he won't sit back and let me suffer for long?

He killed for me.

He brought me here to protect me.

And the look in his eyes when he asked why I hadn't come to *him* for help...

I sink onto the bed, wrapping my arms around myself. The darkness presses in, and I can feel my resolve wavering. But I think of Steven, of all the times I gave in, all the times I let someone else control me. Not this time.

"I can do this," I whisper to myself. "I have to do this."

CHAPTER 15
LUCIEN

"You gave her the pills? Her clothes?" Kim is leaning on the edge of my desk. He watches me storm into the room and go straight for the decanter of blood on the sideboard.

"She refused to take them."

"The clothes?" Kim frowns.

"The pills," I bark, downing a glass then pouring another.

"Why?"

I stalk to the computer and turn on the feed to the bedroom. She has moved the tray onto the floor, pushed it up against the armchair so she doesn't bump into it, and is feeling around on the bed for her clothes.

I watch her take off her jeans and her underwear.

She is completely naked.

"Lucien?" Kim taps the top of the screen, demanding my attention. "Why wouldn't she take them?"

"She says she won't take them until I tell her why she's really here."

I meet Kim's eyes. He smiles and nods approvingly. "Clever girl," he mutters. Then he nods at me. "She got the measure of you quickly, didn't she? She's been here less than twenty-four hours and she's already worked out that she's your Achilles heel."

"Tell me about the vampires at the house." I force myself to stop watching her. Even though she's bending over the bed, using it to steady herself as she steps into a fresh pair of underwear, exposing her ass in a way that practically makes me salivate.

Kim's expression turns serious. He runs a hand through his hair, a habit he has when he's about to deliver bad news.

"It was a mess, Lucien. Two vampires. They ransacked the place, looking for something. When I confronted the younger one, an older one showed up."

I tear my gaze away from the screen, giving Kim my full attention. "And?"

"The young one said something. 'He will destroy you... all of you.' Before I could get more, the older vamp staked him."

My fist clenches around my glass. "And the older one?"

Kim's jaw tightens. "Staked himself. Said I'd get no answers and just... ended it."

"He killed himself rather than expose whoever sent them there." I down the rest of my drink, processing this information. For a vampire to kill themselves takes extreme strength. It goes against our very nature. We are wired for survival at all costs. "They were looking for something. What?"

"No idea. But—" Kim hesitates, moving around to my side of the desk and glancing at the screen where Luna is now fully dressed, sitting on the edge of the bed. "There's more. At the bookshop this morning, when you sent me to clean up, I felt something. Something I've never encountered before."

I raise an eyebrow, encouraging him to continue.

"I didn't tell you before because I didn't understand it. But it was powerful. Ancient. And hungry." Kim shivers at the memory. "I saw things in the mirror. Shadows moving where they shouldn't. It was like the place was alive with some kind of energy."

I lean back in my chair, steepling my fingers. "And?"

Kim meets my eyes, his expression grave. "I hate to say it, but I think you might be right. About Luna. About her connection to the Covenant."

I nod slowly, a mix of vindication and dread settling in my stomach. "So now you understand why she can't leave. Why she needs to be protected."

"Yeah," Kim says, looking back at the screen where Luna sits in darkness. "I get it now. But Lucien... some of the energy I've felt is dark. Incrediblty powerful. So, are you protecting her or are you protecting everyone else *from* her?"

I don't answer. Because honestly, I'm not sure I know the answer myself.

∼

WHEN KIM LEAVES, I settle in for a long night of watching Luna. There is nothing else we can do tonight, and if I'm going to make use of him tomorrow, he needs sleep.

He is human, after all.

I pour another glass of blood and stare at the screen. The darkness doesn't impede my vampire vision, and I see every painful moment of her stubbornness.

She tosses and turns, unable to find a comfortable position. Her face contorts with pain, and I can almost feel it radiating through the screen. She tries lying on her back, then her side, then curled up in a fetal position. Nothing seems to work. Her hands clutch at the sheets, knuckles white with tension.

Hours pass, and she doesn't sleep. Instead, she curls into herself, trembling. I watch as she presses her palms against her temples, massaging in small circles as if trying to ward off dark thoughts. Her lips move silently – is she counting? Reciting something to herself? Whatever it is, it doesn't seem to help.

Occasionally, she sits up abruptly as if struck by a sudden jolt of pain. She rocks back and forth, arms wrapped tightly around her knees. The motion is almost hypnotic, a desperate attempt at self-soothing.

When the first sob escapes her lips, it's like a knife to my chest. It starts as a small, choked sound, barely audible. But soon, it grows into full-blown weeping. I grip the edge of my desk, knuckles white, as I watch her cry. Each tear feels like it's tearing me apart.

I killed a man for making her cry like this. And now I am the monster destroying her beautiful soul.

She buries her face in her pillow, muffling her cries. Her shoulders shake with the force of her sobs. Between bouts of crying, she gasps for air, her breath coming in short, sharp pants. It's as if the pain is stealing the very oxygen from her lungs.

I want to go to her, to hold her, to make the pain stop. But I can't. Not until she understands that she needs to trust me to figure all this out.

As dawn approaches, Luna finally moves. She's been lying still for the past hour, staring blankly at the ceiling. Now, she stumbles in the darkness, feeling her way to the bathroom. Her movements are slow, cautious, each step seeming to cost her great effort. I lean forward, frustrated by the lack of camera there. Minutes tick by, and she doesn't emerge. Ten minutes. Twenty. Thirty.

Finally, the bathroom door opens. Luna steps out, skin damp, hair loose over her shoulders, towel wrapped around her. In one hand, she's holding her pills. In the other... is that a razor?

I lean closer and watch her sit on the edge of the bed. She spends a long time just sitting there, staring at her hands even though she can't see them.

She shifts, and the towel rides up.

There is something on her thigh.

Are those scars?

Ice cold dread thickens instantly in my veins.

Luna presses the razor to her inner thigh. She screws her eyes closed, takes it away, bites her lower lip. She taps her foot, her toes curl.

The realization of what she's thinking of doing to herself hits me like a physical blow.

I'm out of my chair and running before I even register moving.

CHAPTER 16
LUNA

The razor feels unnaturally heavy in my hand. But the pills do, too. Both are tantalizingly familiar.

The blade offers me a momentary release.

So do the drugs.

If I open my skin and feel the blood trickle down my leg, I will experience the rush of dopamine that is so very addictive. I will take back control of my emotions.

But it will not last, and the come down, the guilt, the shame, will be almost unbearable.

The pills do not carry the same risks. I hate that I depend on them. But they are meant to help me not hurt me.

That is what I am telling myself as I stare at them.

I run my finger over the foil packet. The temptation to hear the 'pop' the foil makes when I free the pill is almost unbearable. My body aches with need for it.

But *not* taking them is the only control I have over him.

Lucien.

In the dark, I close my eyes and visualize the razor and the pills and how they look in my pale aching hands. One allows me to claim some control over my emotions. The other offers control over my circumstances.

But if I *don't* take the pills, I will be in too much pain to even contemplate finding a way out of here.

I am still trying to make my choice when the bedroom door clatters open. Lights flicker to life, but they are muted and cast a dim glow instead of a powerful illumination.

Still, I blink to adjust my eyes.

Lucien is standing in the doorway, breathing hard. Chest rising and falling. He strides toward me, slamming the door closed as he moves.

"What are you doing with that?" He points at the razor.

Looking at it now, seeing it in my palm, I'm not sure whether I am more or less tempted to use it.

Before I can answer, he snatches it from me and throws it across the room. It meets the wall with such force the plastic handle snaps in two.

"Take the pills," he says.

I tighten my fist around the pill packet. "Tell me why I'm here. Why I'm *really* here. Then I'll take them."

"You are in pain." He growls and takes hold of my wrist. "Take the pills."

Staring up at him, tears fill my eyes. I try to blink them away, but I can't. I look away from him. His grip loosens, and he moves away from me.

When he returns, he's holding a glass of water.

I let him take the packet from my hand and free two pills. When he presses them back into my palm, he holds the glass to my lips.

Suddenly, every ounce of fight is gone.

I do not argue.

My body is pleading with me to give in.

The pain is too much.

I place them onto my tongue and let him feed me a drink of water to swallow them down with.

Lucien sighs, and nods at me as if he is truly incredibly relieved.

"Why do you care if I take them?" I whisper.

"Because I cannot watch you in pain." His words are gentle, but his tone is not. Like he cannot stand the fact he cares about my discomfort.

He glances down at my thighs, then over at the razor that now lies in pieces on the floor.

Uncomfortable, I press my legs together.

How did he know?

Once again, the idea that he has been watching me flits into my mind, but it almost instantly dissolves and floats away because Lucien is getting down on his knees in front of me.

As I watch him, he reaches out with torturously slow hands. I wince as his touch meets my legs.

I never let anyone see this part of me. I keep my scars covered. Always.

Steven saw them, and he was appalled. His eyes grew dark, and he tutted, and told me never to let him see them again.

After that, we had sex in the dark. I showered with the door locked and made sure I was fully covered by a towel before I entered the bedroom.

I look down at Lucien. His eyes meet mine as he catches the hem of the towel and slides it further up my legs. Over my thighs until I am fully exposed.

My skin is still damp, still warm, and I am not wearing any underwear.

He parts my legs, and exhales slowly. Then he takes his hand

and moves it over my inner thigh. His palm levitates above my skin. He does not touch me, but the change in pressure of the air between us makes me shudder.

When he does touch me, it is with one finger only. He traces each scar slowly, and I watch him transfixed.

"Did you do this to yourself kitten?" he breathes.

I nod, unable to speak.

His eyes flash with anger, but not the anger that Steven showed me. Lucien's anger is different. He is not ashamed of me or of the scars. He is angry that I felt the need to do this to myself.

He does not ask me why.

He just moves slowly closer, still on his knees in front of me.

His hands slide round to hold my hips, and he fixes his gaze on mine. "When did you last hurt yourself?" he asks.

I swallow hard. I want to tell him I haven't done it for years, but that would be a lie.

"A month ago." I point to my ankle. The faint outline of a cut from a razor blade is just about visible.

He cups my heel with both hands and lifts my foot to his mouth, then kisses it. My ankle. The scar.

I close my eyes, and a soft murmur parts my lips.

But then he lowers my foot back to the floor and meets my eyes again. "You were thinking about hurting yourself here? In my house?"

"It makes me feel... in control." I have never tried to explain to anyone before.

Lucien's jaw twitches. He licks his fangs.

This time, firmly, he says, "You will never hurt yourself again." He holds my gaze, and I simply cannot look away.

Something in his voice makes me nod, breathless, tingling all over.

His grip tightens on my hips.

"You need to hurt something, you hurt me." He grabs my hand, takes my fingers, and drags my nails down his throat so that three red scratch marks appear. A tiny bead of blood appears on his skin, then disappears almost instantly.

"You need to *feel* something, you come to me."

He kisses me. Deeply. His tongue caresses mine, and I moan into his mouth.

When he pulls away, he holds my face with one large, strong hand. "Do you understand, kitten?"

I nod again, trembling at the way the nickname *kitten* feels as it lands on my skin.

Lucien stands up and tweaks his finger under my chin. "You will never disrespect your body again. Am I making myself clear, Luna?"

"Yes," I whisper.

"Yes, what?"

"Yes, Lucien." The words tumble from my lips, and his eyes flash. He grabs my face. His lips slam into mine. When he pulls away, leaving me breathless, he says, "How do you feel now? Do you feel in control?"

I shake my head.

"Do you need to hurt something?"

I don't know what I need. I feel out of control but not in the way I normally do. I feel like I want to give myself to him. Every bit. And let him do what he wants with me. Like I want him to make me feel so much that I feel nothing at all.

"No. Not now." I reach for his belt, tuck my thumbs into it and stare up at him. "I need something else."

CHAPTER 17
LUNA

His mouth drops open a little. I can see the outline of his cock through the fabric of his pants. I lean forward and rest my cheek against it, stroking it with one hand while the other snakes around to grab his ass.

He groans, and it sounds like sin laced with treacle.

He leans into my touch. I open my mouth and gently bite him through the fabric. "Fuck," he murmurs.

The power and dominance in his voice sends shivers down my spine. I am his, and he knows it. I have finally agreed to give myself completely to him, to let him lead me into the darkest corners of desire. And right now, I can barely contain my excitement.

He lowers his head to mine and our lips meet once again, this time with a hunger I have never experienced before. His tongue slides into my mouth, exploring every inch, and I moan softly, my hands tangled in his hair. I can feel his arousal growing harder against me.

I pull away from him and stare up into his eyes. His gaze is intense. "Will it please you to touch me?" he asks.

Instinctively, I nod.

But then he grasps my chin, and his eyes darken. "Will it please you?" he asks me again in a tone that makes me sit back a little and blink up at him.

"If touching me gives you pleasure, I welcome it," he breathes. "If taking my cock in your mouth and feeling me in your throat will make you wet, and send shivers to your beautiful pussy, then I welcome it." He moves closer, so there is barely any distance between us now.

"But you will not do anything just because you think it is what I want from you. Is that clear?"

"Yes." My voice is barely there at all. Arousal constricts in my chest and between my legs.

"Then I will ask you again. Will it please you?" He stares at me, and I feel as though I will never *ever* be able to lie to him. As if he will know it the second an untruth passes my lips.

In response, I drop to my knees before him, my hands shaking with anticipation. "Just the thought of it pleases me."

Lucien sighs and closes his eyes.

As I undo his pants, I can feel the room getting warmer. Like our bodies are already generating enough heat to fuel a furnace.

His cock is hard, and thick, and I find myself thinking that it is beautiful.

I study him for a moment, then I reach out and take him in my hand, stroking him slowly, savoring the feel of him in my palm.

Instinctively, I spit into my hand and use it to moisten his shaft.

I look up, and Lucien's gaze collides with mine.

He is watchin me as if he has never seen anything so wonderful.

No one has ever looked at me like that.

He places one gentle hand on the back of my head but does not push me toward him. Just leaves it there as if he is reassuring me that I'm doing a good job.

I open my mouth and lick a slow, delicious line from the base of his cock to the tip. Then I swirl my tongue around him, tasting the first salty drop of pleasure.

He moans loudly, then mutters my name. Our eyes lock, and I can see the fire in his. Small sparkling freckles of crimson that dance in his gaze as he stares at me.

I slide a hand down between my legs.

He watches me for a moment, but when I start to move faster, he grabs my chin and stops me. "Not yet, kitten," he says. "It is my job to make you purr."

He pulls me up with a gentle force, and I follow his lead, my heart pounding, my body tingling with an almost unbearable heat.

His hand moves to my chest. His fingers trace the top of the bath towel to where it is tucked beneath my arm. Slowly, he flicks the fabric so it falls to the floor.

He stands back and admires me.

That is the only word for it... admiration.

And instead of feeling like I need to cover myself up, I let him stare. I watch his eyes trail over my breasts, my stomach, the swell of my hips, the roundness of my thighs. He signals with his finger for me to turn around.

I move in a slow circle, allowing him to see every last inch of my body.

When I am facing him again, he tells me to sit down.

"Right there, on the edge," he says. But then he frowns. "Would you be more comfortable lying down?"

I open my mouth to reply but the answer quivers on my

tongue. Why is it so hard to ask for what I want? Even when he is offering it to me? Why do I feel afraid to say the wrong thing? Even to a man who means nothing to me?

He doesn't need me to answer. He scoops me effortlessly into his arms and sets me down in the middle of the bed. He props me up on the pillows then takes one and positions it under my lower back. I wriggle down just a little, and he smiles.

A real smile. As if he is truly pleased I am comfortable.

"Would you take off your clothes?" The question leaves my mouth before I have time to think about it. When Lucien smirks at me, I smile back. "I want to see you," I whisper. "All of you."

He is standing at the foot of the bed now. Nodding, he slides his black braces off his shoulders, then unfastens his shirt. When he takes it off, I feel my eyes widen. I sink back a little onto the pillows, staring at him.

His arms are toned and muscular, his chest and shoulders broad and perfectly sculpted. And there is the exact right amount of dark, tantalizing hair peppering his stomach. Leading down to his waistband, where his fingers are unfastening his belt.

Dropping his pants to the floor, he steps out of them and allows me to stare a moment longer before he crawls onto the bed and eases open my legs.

I stare down at him, amazed by the look of excitement on his face.

He holds my thighs apart, gently but with a strength that makes my breath catch in my chest.

He is so much stronger than me, and the fact he is so very aware of having to be gentle with my body makes my head spin; he is not just aware of it, he is putting my comfort and pleasure above his own.

And that is something I have never experienced before.

Something I never even knew existed.

"Fuck, Luna..." He traces one finger over my wet, sensitive core. "Do you know how many times I've thought about this?"

He looks up at me and the intense, piercing, eye contact makes me gasp. He keeps staring at me while he kisses my inner thighs, drawing slow deliberate patterns on my skin.

He lets out a low growl and flashes his fangs at me.

Does he want to bite me? Is he contemplating it right now? Sinking his teeth into my flesh and sucking, and sucking.

He reaches the scars that tell the story of my pain.

I remember each one.

I remember what I was feeling, and how much I was hurting.

And he kisses them. One by one — pressing his lips to them, then stroking with soft fingers as if he might be able to erase them. Or make them mean something else. Something beautiful.

He rests his cheek on the inside of my thigh and strokes me for the longest time.

Not my pussy.

Everything *except* my pussy.

His hands roam my legs, my hips, my stomach.

Then finally, when I am whimpering for his touch on my clit, he presses his lips to it and begins to suck.

I feel the vibrations in my core as he uses his tongue and his mouth to explore me.

It is as if he is reading my sounds, and my movements. When I moan, he gives me more. If I tilt my hips toward him, he gives me more.

He is fast, and slow, and hard, and soft, and everything in between.

I arch my back, my hips bucking as I feel his tongue dancing on my sensitive spots, his fingers teasing the edges of my pussy.

I grab his hair, and he looks up at me with a mischievous smile.

"I need your fingers inside me." I plead with him.

He obliges immediately, hooking two fingers inside and moving them in tandem with his tongue.

Pleasure ricochets through me.

It is almost unbearable.

"Please, don't stop." I am grinding my hips, gripping the pillows. My whole body is on fire, and my skin is laced with sweat.

He knows I'm close, that I can't hold back any longer. He keeps the same rhythm, doesn't change it or slow down or speed up. I cry out in pleasure. He laps at me, his tongue flicking against my clit and sending shockwaves through my body.

I can feel the pleasure building inside me. It is going to consume me at any moment. My breath hitches. I bunch my fist and slam it into the mattress while Lucien continues his relentless assault, his lips and tongue working together to unleash the most intense orgasm I've ever experienced.

As I come, my entire body trembles. It coils tighter and tighter, and as the wave of pleasure subsides, sweeping back through my limbs, my muscles weaken. My eyes roll, and all I can do is lie back on the pillows, panting, unable to think about anything except the way he made me feel.

Lucien nibbles the inside of my thigh. He stokes me gently, then uses his tongue to clean my wetness. This time, though, he is not trying to turn me on. He is soft and tender.

When he sits up, kneeling in front of me, his cock is glistening with precum, and he is touching himself.

I bite my lower lip and smile at him. "Thank you," I whisper.

"You are exquisite when you come," he replies, fist still wrapped around his swollen shaft.

"I'd like to know what you look like when you come." I sit up, deliberately keeping my legs open. I slide my hand between my legs. "And I'd like to know if watching you will turn me on enough to make me come again."

CHAPTER 18

LUNA

Lucien's eyes darken with lust. He crawls up the bed, his cock inches away from my entrance. Then he hesitates. His expression changes. "I don't want to hurt you."

Smiling, giggling a little, I look down at his cock. "You're big, Lucien, but you're not *that* big."

Still staring at me, he slides his hands up my outer thighs and grips my hips, dimpling them with his fingers. I have realized that whenever I make him laugh, he is surprised by it. And the look on his face – like he'd forgotten how to find anything funny and is surprised I am talking to him the way I am – makes a strange, warm sense of affection settle in my belly.

"That is not what I meant." He moves one hand to his shaft again. When he curls his fingers around it, I bite my lower lip and my hips instinctively tilt toward him, heat pooling in my core even though my clit is still sensitive and throbbing.

Still touching himself, Lucien watches me start to stroke my pussy.

"I want to fuck you, Luna. But I'm a vampire. I'm strong. And when I'm inside you I'm going to be incredibly turned on. What if I make it worse?"

"The pain?" Shame and embarrassment wash over me. I stop touching myself and sit back a little.

As I move, Lucien moves with me. "Explain it to me."

My eyes fill with tears, and I hate that I'm *that* girl who's crying in bed with a hot guy. "It never goes away. It's always there."

"So, when I'm touching you...?" He is resting his hands gently on my knees now, stroking me with his fingertips.

I laugh and shake my head. I don't want to talk about this. I don't want it here, intruding on this moment. For once, I want to feel like the girl who can do what she likes. Whose body will do what she commands. I try to bring him toward me, using my legs to pull him closer but he resists.

"Talk to me," he says, a command and a plea at the same time.

"Pain isn't sexy, Lucien."

"Everything about you is sexy."

I shake my head again. "Even when you're touching me, it's still there. And tomorrow, I'll feel like I've run a marathon, been run over by a truck, and thrown headfirst over a cliff because my body just can't allow me to feel *good*." My voice cracks and I feel like I need to reach for a blanket and cover myself up. "I'm weak."

"You are the strongest person I have ever met." He tries to smile. "And I've been alive a long time. I've met a lot of humans."

A tear escapes and rolls down my cheek. "Please, fuck me."

"I can't hurt you." He pushes his fingers through his hair.

"Fuck me, Lucien." I sit up and take his hand, then tug it gently, forcing him to lie above me. "However I'm going to feel tomorrow, it will be worth it." I meet his eyes and feel my tears turn to something more determined. "This is my choice. I need to control this. Let me control this."

I tighten my grip on him with my thighs. His lips collide with mine.

And before I can say anything else, he slides inside me.

The intensity of the pleasure makes me gasp. He is large and hard, and it takes me a moment to adjust to the sensation of being so full.

He kisses me again as he moves in and out of my aching body.

I expect him to be too strong, too hard, too fast, but he is holding back. His movements are controlled.

"Harder." I slip my hand between us and rub my clit, watching his shoulders ripple as he holds my free hand above my head then kisses my neck.

He changes pace. Does as I've asked.

Heat and pleasure dance on my skin and become a new kind of pain. A torment. A frustration. An explosion that's building and building inside me, coiling around my limbs, making my eyes roll back and my breath hitch and my toes curl.

He lifts my legs a little, tilts his pelvis, and starts hitting the spot that make stars explode behind my eyelids.

"I want to see your face," I moan into his ear. "I want to watch your face."

He obliges, sitting up so he can see all of me.

Normally, I'd feel totally exposed like this but the way he is staring at me makes me feel like a goddess.

"Fuck, you look beautiful, kitten."

His eyes trail down my body. He looks as if he might devour me whole. His hips slam into mine, and the bed creaks beneath us both.

I cry out but tell him not to stop.

I close my eyes, but when I open them again, he is holding his wrist against his mouth. I am still touching myself when he bites down on the vein and pierces it with his fangs.

Blood trickles down his arm and onto my stomach. He wraps his other arm around me and lifts me so I'm sitting in his lap. I curl my legs around him. He is still inside me, but now he's offering me his bleeding wrist.

"Drink. My blood will do more for your pain than those pills will ever do." He meets my eyes. Inky pools of salvation.

I shouldn't do this.

I shouldn't *want* to do this. But the thought of having his blood inside me is so overwhelmingly powerful that I can't stop myself.

I grab his hand and seal my lips over the open wound.

When I start to suck, Lucien groans and thrusts into me harder.

His warmth fills my mouth, coats my tongue. Metallic but oddly sweet. It drips onto my chin.

"Luna..." Lucien gasps my name like a prayer, his jaw clenched tightly as he watches me. Then he cups my face in his hand and eases my lips from him. "That's enough now, kitten."

I am panting. My body is on fire.

A gentle warmth begins to spread through my body, starting as a tingle in my throat.

The constant ache I've grown accustomed to doesn't disappear entirely, but it softens around the edges. It's as if someone has turned down the volume on my pain, from a blaring roar to a more manageable hum. The sharp twinges in my joints are suddenly duller, less insistent.

As I wrap my arms around him and grind my pelvis down onto him, I realize my limbs feel different, too. Lighter. When I roll my shoulders and tilt my head back so he can lick the blood from my chin and my throat, the familiar stiffness is there, but muted.

Energy trickles through me, not a surge but a gentle stream.

For the first time in years, I feel a glimmer of what it might be like to live without constant pain.

Pleasure builds inside me. No longer fighting to rise above my pain, it rips effortlessly through my body, and I start to shake. Sweat beads on my shoulders and between my breasts. Darkness swells in the corners of my vision. Lucien holds me tighter, and fucks me harder, and when I climax, I dig my nails into his back and hold onto him as if I might dissolve completely if I didn't have him to keep me here.

As Lucien watches me come, his entire body tenses up. He groans loudly, and the sound increases my pleasure. He stares at me, thrusts harder, then stops. His warmth fills me, hot and beautiful.

I expect him to pull away, but he doesn't.

He stays inside me, stroking my back, holding me tightly against his chest.

I notice that my hips aren't aching, and my back isn't either, and when he lowers me down onto the bed, I slip into a deep, easy sleep.

CHAPTER 19
LUCIEN

Luna sleeps peacefully beside me, her chest rising and falling in a gentle rhythm. I watch her, unable to look away, my mind a whirlwind of conflicting thoughts and emotions.

I replay the events of the night in my head. The way she arched beneath me, her soft gasps of pleasure, the feel of her skin against mine. And then, that moment — her climax building, her body tensing, and suddenly the shadows in the room coming alive. They danced and swirled, responding to her in a way I've only read about in ancient texts.

She is powerful. More powerful than I initially believed. And I've just fed her my blood.

Stupid. Reckless. Dangerous.

I run a hand through my hair, frustration building. What was I thinking? I don't fully understand what she is, what latent abilities might be inside her. And now I've introduced vampire blood to the equation. The potential consequences are unpredictable at best, catastrophic at worst.

My gaze falls on her sleeping form again. She looks so peaceful now, free from the pain that had been etched into her features earlier. Part of me wants to believe that's why I did it — to ease her suffering, to give her a reprieve from the constant agony.

But I can't lie to myself. Not completely. The desire I felt for her was overwhelming, all-consuming. I wanted her so badly, wanted to lose myself in her without worrying about causing her more pain. Was that the real reason? Did I prioritize my own selfish desires over her safety?

I clench my fist, anger at myself rising. I'm supposed to be protecting her, not potentially putting her in more danger. What if my blood awakens something in her that she's not ready to control? What if it draws even more attention from those who might wish to exploit her power?

And yet... I can't bring myself to regret it entirely. The connection I felt with her, the way she responded to me — it was unlike anything I've experienced in my long existence.

I gently brush a strand of hair from her face, marveling at how young and vulnerable she looks in sleep. The urge to protect her, to keep her safe from all harm, wells up inside me with surprising intensity.

But what if I am the one Luna needs protection from?

I rise from the bed, careful not to disturb her, and begin pacing the room. My feelings for her are far more complex than I ever anticipated. What started as an obsession, a need to protect and possess, has evolved into something more. Something I can barely comprehend let alone name.

And instead of dealing with more pressing matters – the vampires that are running riot in the city, and whoever the fuck is controlling them, and whether that person knows what she is – I'm here, losing myself in her.

I sit down in the armchair and watch her sleeping. How many

times have I dreamed of watching her like this? Of being close to her? Of seeing her come while I'm inside her? Feeling her clench around me, and hearing her scream my name?

Now, here she is.

But I do not deserve the pleasure she makes me feel.

After everything I've done, after all these centuries of guarding my heart, how can I allow myself to be this vulnerable again?

I close my eyes. Memories rise from the basement of my soul, sharp and painful. And I let them come for me.

~

ENGLAND, 1521

I stand in the shadows of our bedchamber, watching Elizabeth sleep.

For weeks, I've managed to hide my new nature from her. I have fed in secret, convincing myself that I could find a way to return to my life. That I could still be the man she married.

"Lucien?" Her voice, soft with sleep, pulls me from my thoughts. "You're home late again."

I move to her side, taking her hand in mine. Even in the dim candlelight, I can see the concern in her eyes. "I'm sorry, my love. There was business to attend to."

She sits up, her brow furrowing. "You're so cold. Are you ill?"

"No, I'm fine," I assure her, fighting the urge to recoil as her warm hand touches my cheek. Trying to ignore the throbbing vein in her neck, visible beneath her pale skin.

The scent of her blood is intoxicating, and I hate myself for noticing it.

A growl rises in my throat, and I try to bite down on it.

I kiss her neck and pull her closer. But I'm too rough. She jerks away from me and studies my face.

"Your eyes... Lucien, what's happened to you?"

I try to explain, to make her understand. I tell her everything — the ambush, the vampire who turned me, stories that sound as though they're something from a gruesome fairy tale instead of from our reality. Through it all, she listens in horrified silence.

When I finish, I reach for her hand. "But my love for you hasn't changed. We can still be together, Elizabeth. I'll find a way. I will fight what they made me. I swear to you—"

The sting of holy water hits my face before I can react. Elizabeth stands at the edge of the bed, clutching a small vial.

"Demon," she hisses. "You're not my husband."

She scrambles from the bed, trips and falls into the dresser. Her head is bleeding. She raises her hand to touch the wound. Blood coats her fingers.

Her eyes widen. She looks at me and shakes her head. "Please, Lucien. No."

But in that moment, all my control, all my humanity, slips away. I move without thinking, my hand closing around her throat.

It's over in seconds.

I sink my teeth into her neck and drink until there is nothing left.

I don't try to turn her. I don't know how.

I let her slip away from me and stare at her lifeless body as it crumples onto the floor. And while I stare at her... I feel nothing.

Nothing except the need to feed again.

∽

Luna stirs in her sleep. She murmurs something and the sound of her voice drags me back to the present.

She sits up in bed, stretching her arms out sideways as if she has had the most peaceful sleep of her life. When she sees me, she smiles, and my dark mood lifts.

I hate that it lifts from looking at her.

Being with her.

I hate that even though I know love leads to nothing but pain and betrayal, I can feel myself falling for her.

I should send her away from this place. But I can't because I need to keep her safe the way I need air to breathe and blood to feed on. It is an unquestionable part of my being now.

She is a part of my being.

"I'm suddenly absolutely starving," she says, reaching for her glasses. As she slips them onto the bridge of her nose, she yawns and holds one hand over her stomach. It grumbles loudly.

"Pasta." I gesture to the tray. "I brought it last night."

She nods and motions for me to bring it to her, sitting up and folding her legs beneath the bedsheets.

I set the tray down and watch as she levers a forkful of food into her mouth.

"Coffee?"

She tilts her head at me.

"I can have some coffee brought up. If you'd like some."

She frowns as if she's confused by my overly formal way of addressing her all of a sudden. "Coffee would be good. Do you have staff for that?"

I find my phone, in my pants pocket on the floor by the fireplace, and text Trent. *If you're awake, bring coffee, milk, and sugar to Luna's room.*

He was dubious about me bringing her here. But he's also curious, so I know he'll obey my request. Desperate to catch a glimpse of the woman who is so important she has to be locked inside my house for her own safety.

"Not staff, exactly."

Luna wipes her mouth with the back of her hand. "I'm guessing you don't eat?"

"I can if I want to, but it always feels a little pointless." I pull my pants on and sit down on the edge of the bed.

She bites her lower lip, then glances at my wrist. "It's healed already."

"It has." I am shirtless and notice her gaze moving to my chest. "How do you feel?"

Her nose wrinkles. She puts down the fork and moves the tray to one side. "Lighter," she says." As if I've taken a quadruple dose of my meds."

"I'm glad it helped you."

"You really are glad, aren't you?" she asks, reaching for my hand.

The gesture is intimate and soft and makes me feel like I should stand up and jerk away from her. But as her fingers slot between mine and she smiles at me, I can't ignore the desire to just be in her presence. Like this.

I'm about to kiss her again, pull the sheets away from her body and trail kisses down her throat, when there's a knock on the door. I open it to find Trent holding a cafetière in one hand and two mugs in the other. A carton of milk is tucked under his arm and a packet of sugar protrudes from him jeans pocket. He looks exhausted, and it occurs to me I have no idea what time it is.

"You'd make a terrible butler," I grumble, letting him inside so he can set down the cafetière on the coffee table.

"Sorry, boss. I didn't realize you were entertaining, or I'd have used the posh silverware." He casts a too-long glance in Luna's direction. I sense his muscles tense. He flicks his gaze over her face, her body, even though it's hidden beneath the sheets, and she draws her legs up to her chest uncomfortably.

Anger flares in my gut.

I slam my hand around his throat and have him pinned against the wall before he can whimper, "What did I do, boss?"

"You don't look at her like that. Ever." My face is inches from his. "In fact. You don't look at her. You don't *think* about her. She is under my protection and mine alone. If I catch you so much as breathing in her direction again, I'll personally ensure you never see another full moon. Do I make myself clear?"

Trent nods quickly. "Of course, boss. It won't happen again."

I lean in closer, my voice barely above a whisper. "See that it doesn't. Remember, I can smell your thoughts. Keep them pure or keep them nonexistent when it comes to her. Understood?"

"Yes, boss," Trent replies, visibly shaken.

I know I'm overreacting. But I also know that Luna's pulse has quickened and that she's watching me right now.

And I need her to see this.

I need her to know I meant it when I said I would protect her.

He made her uncomfortable.

He won't do it again.

"Good. Now get back to your post. And spread the word — Luna is off limits to everyone but me."

CHAPTER 20
KIM

The Crimson Moon isn't the kind of place I usually frequent, but tonight, I need information more than I need sleep. The bar caters to Cambridge's supernatural crowd - a dingy, underground joint where vampires, werewolves, and other creatures of the night can drink without fear of exposure.

I push through the heavy wooden door, immediately assaulted by the smell of stale beer and something metallic that I try not to think too hard about. The bar is dimly lit, shadows dancing on the walls from flickering candles. It's busy for a weeknight, a low hum of conversation punctuated by occasional bursts of laughter.

I make my way to the bar, sliding onto a stool and catching the bartender's eye. He's a tall, lean man with unnaturally pale skin and eyes that gleam red in the low light. Definitely a vampire. Thankfully, he doesn't know what I am.

"What'll it be?" he asks, voice gravelly.

"Whiskey, neat," I reply, trying to look like I belong here.

As he pours my drink, I casually glance around the room. There's a mix of patrons - some clearly vampires, others with the wild, barely contained energy of werewolves. In the corner, a group of what look like witches huddle over a table, whispering intently.

The bartender slides my drink over. I take a sip, letting the burn of the alcohol steady my nerves.

"You're new here," the bartender says. It's not a question.

I shrug, aiming for nonchalance. "Just passing through. Heard this was the place to be if you're... not exactly human."

He nods slowly, eyes narrowing slightly. "That it is. Though things have been a bit unsettled lately."

I raise an eyebrow, feigning casual interest. "Oh? How so?"

The bartender leans in, lowering his voice. "Word is, there's been a change in management. The old boss who ran the FHB trade? Gone. Poof." He snaps his fingers for emphasis.

"Really?" I take another sip of whiskey. "Any idea who's taken over?"

He shakes his head. "That's the thing. No one knows. But whoever it is, they're shaking things up. Prices are up, quality's down, and there's talk of expanding beyond Cambridge."

I frown, processing this information. "Sounds like bad news for everyone."

The bartender nods grimly. "You have no idea. Last guy who asked too many questions about it? Found him drained dry in an alley."

A chill runs down my spine, but I keep my face neutral. "Thanks for the heads up. I'll keep that in mind."

As I finish my drink, a commotion breaks out near the door. Two vampires, young and clearly high on FHB, are arguing loudly. The bartender sighs, moving out from behind the bar to deal with it.

I take the opportunity to slip away, my mind racing. A new boss, expanding operations, and willing to kill to keep it quiet?

After what Lucien did to the queen, who would dare to challenge him? And how does Luna fit into it?

I really should sleep. But I know all that will happen if I go home now will be a restless night, thoughts tumbling. I also know that if I go home, I'll start thinking about Sarah.

～

By the time I reach the mansion, it's morning. I didn't go home, but I did drive around the city trying to sift through the mess of thoughts in my head.

I text Lucien several times with no reply, which is unusual given that he's usually awake all night. But perhaps not unusual given that he has Luna to occupy him.

When I buzz the gate, there is no answer. So, I abandon the Volvo and climb over the wall.

If you'd told me a year ago, when I was working for a regular marketing firm in the city center, still pretending to be a regular human, that I'd be strong enough or brave enough to scale the wall of a vampire's mansion, I'd have laughed.

It took me a *long* time to accept my destiny. And I hate that word with a passion. It sounds like something from a bad superhero movie.

Even when demons were tracking me down, trying to kill me before I killed them because they could *sense* my hunter blood, I ignored what was happening.

I ran away to start a new life in sleepy Cambridge. I brought Sarah with me, thinking I could shield her from it and that she'd never have to know what I really was.

And then she died.

Because of the exact thing I was trying to protect her from.

Don't think it hasn't occurred to me that I'm getting caught up in Lucien's desire to protect Luna because she reminds me of my dead wife.

I'm no back-seat therapist but I've watched enough social media reels to know I'm playing out the same scenario and hoping for a different result this time.

Vulnerable woman. Looks spookily like the woman I loved. Needs protection from evil forces... count me in! Maybe I can redeem myself by saving her.

Just because I'm aware of what I'm doing, though, doesn't mean I have the wherewithal to stop it.

I've barely put a foot on the ground when Lucien's dogs appear. Four Doberman that look like they're ready to tear me limb from limb. I fold my arms and tap my foot, staring at them.

Rex, the biggest, drops to the floor and rolls over like a puppy. The others stop too, wagging their tails.

Dogs love me. Always have. Even these ones.

"Come on. Let's find your master." I gesture to the house and the dogs run alongside me as if they're out for a playdate not protecting their property from potential assailants.

The house is in almost total darkness. Not unusual for Lucien. But the aura that I felt earlier is back, and it's stronger now.

Above me, the sky is brightening. It's going to be another cold, crisp day. Strange that we've had so many in a row. Surely, any minute now the rain will return; it wouldn't feel like England in February without it.

I push on the front door, and it swings open.

Half expecting Trent to appear from nowhere, I brace myself to be startled, but no one is there.

I head straight for Lucien's study, but there is no one here either. Just an empty desk chair, pushed back against the wall, a half-drunk glass of blood, and a glowing computer screen.

He left in a hurry.

I move to the desk to see whether he left his phone, then notice movement on the screen. I peer at it, then realize I'm looking at Luna's bedroom. And that her and Lucien are sitting in bed together, drinking coffee.

Did he spend the night with her?

Did they...?

I examine the buttons on screen and skip back through the feed. For a while, there is barely any movement, just Luna sleeping and Lucien watching her, his eyes glowing in the darkness.

But then... they are naked. Fucking.

I increase the speed and cycle back faster then hit play.

The room around them is dimly lit. The bed sheets are tangled, and the sound of their heavy breathing makes my own breath catch in my chest. As Luna curls into Lucien's embrace, her body pressed against his chest, legs around him, I sit down in Lucien's chair.

A deep pang of longing for physical contact hits me in my core. Not just contact with anyone, though... contact with *her*.

I study the pair of them. Lucien is holding his wrist to Luna's mouth. He's bleeding. Fuck... he's going to feed her?

I lean forward, gripping the edge of the desk, and watch as she seals her perfect lips around his open flesh. When she starts to suck, and her eyes meet his, my cock stiffens.

Fuck, she looks so good.

The pair of them together look so good.

As Luna drinks, Lucien's rough yet gentle fingers run through her hair, pulling out the pale strands from where they're tangled in her eyes and around her lips. He nuzzles her neck, his fangs grazing her slightly as he does so.

When he sits back, telling her she's had enough and easing her mouth from his skin, his eyes are filled with hunger. But it isn't hunger for blood; it is hunger for her.

He starts to move his hips faster, and she clings onto him, crying his name as he fucks her harder.

They're a mismatched pair – his lean muscular form and rugged features contrasting with Luna's soft frame, but somehow they fit together.

I'm so hard now I can't stand it.

Fumbling with my belt, I unfasten my jeans and thrust my hand into my boxers, pulling out my cock. Already, precum glistens on its tip.

I lightly brush the head of my cock through my palm and allow myself a small groan as I watch them.

I'll admit it, watching has always been my thing. It started with Sarah because we were saving ourselves for marriage. She would tease me, making herself come for me while I stroked myself watching her. Sometimes, in the run up to the wedding, she would send me videos. Her hand slipping below the sheets into her underwear. It became an obsession... the idea of her pleasuring herself.

I have never watched a couple before. But Lucien and Luna? This is something else. This is a level of arousal I haven't felt before, and touching myself doesn't feel like enough.

It is like there is too much distance between us.

I want to be in the room. I want to smell their sweat and their heat. I want to be close enough to see her cheeks flushing and her lip trembling as she bites down on the urge to come.

I lean closer, fisting my cock furiously as I watch them.

With each thrust of Lucien's hips, Luna moans and her body

shudders in response, sending shockwaves of pleasure through my own body. Her nails dig into Lucien's skin, her fingers entwined in his hair as he slams deeper into her, claiming what is his. She throws her head back, panting his name like a prayer.

Lucien's eyes never leave hers as he holds her hips tightly, marking her with his firm grip.

As they move together, my head spins.

Every time he hits the spot inside her that sends shivers down her spine, she gasps and arches under him, hissing out tiny little moans that make me harder and more desperate to come.

I realize I am watching Lucien, too. Almost as much as I'm watching Luna. And now I need to use another hand. This one on my balls.

I picture her crawling beneath the desk and putting them in her mouth.

I picture him fucking her right here in front of me. Bending her over while I watch the two of them just inches from my face.

When she climaxes, he does too.

I am not far behind them.

An orgasm, quick and powerful, makes me slam the desk with my closed fist as ropes of cum spill onto the floor.

I am panting, one hand still on my cock, when I hear a voice down the hall.

Fuck.

Trent.

He's calling for the dogs, but he's coming this way.

CHAPTER 21

LUNA

The rich aroma of coffee fills the air as Lucien pours us both a cup. It's such a normal, domestic act that for a moment, I forget where I am and who he is. As he hands me the steaming mug, our fingers brush, and I feel that now-familiar tingle of electricity.

"Thank you," I murmur, wrapping my hands around the warm ceramic.

We settle into a comfortable silence, and I can't help but marvel at how at ease I feel. It's dangerous, this sense of comfort. I should be on guard, shouldn't I? He's a vampire. A powerful, ancient being who's been keeping me here against my will.

And yet, it feels right. Normal, even. Like something a couple would do the morning after a good date if they'd gone home together and liked each other. The thought makes me blush, and I hide behind my coffee cup.

Lucien's voice breaks the silence. "How's your pain this morning?"

I look up, meeting his concerned gaze. There's genuine care there, and it catches me off guard.

"Better," I admit. "Whatever is in your blood... it helped."

He nods, a small smile playing at the corners of his mouth. "I'm glad. But it will wear off soon."

"I understand."

"I probably shouldn't have offered it to you," he says, more contemplative than annoyed at himself. "Forming a habit would not be a good idea."

"It's okay. I won't pester you for more."

"You wouldn't need to *pester*. I just mean—" Lucien stops when he notices me smiling at him. It is very endearing, the way he can change from being utterly terrifying one minute – like when he was threatening Trent – to almost tender the next. He takes a sip of his coffee. "When did it start? Your illness, I mean. I have to admit, it's not something I fully understand."

I hesitate, my fingers tightening around the mug. It's not something I talk about often, but something tells me he's willing to listen.

"It started after a car accident. It has a stupid long name – fibromyalgia – but apparently, it can be triggered by traumatic, painful events. Or an accumulation of them. Doctors don't really understand it. I think the last consultant I saw said it was something to do with the way my brain processes pain signals. But other doctors have said it's more like ME or Chronic Fatigue." I laugh dryly, rolling my eyes at myself. "I hate talking about this stuff. Like I said, it's not exactly sexy."

"I want to understand." Lucien shifts closer on the bed, then slides a hand beneath the sheets and squeezes the soft flesh above my waist again. "And, like I said, I find everything about you sexy, Luna."

Usually, I'd flinch and pull away. Instead, I let him keep his hand there. "The accident happened when I was in college," I begin, my voice soft. "I was home for the holidays, driving my parents back from my dad's work Christmas party."

Lucien leans forward, his full attention on me. I take a deep breath and continue.

"My dad was drunk, which wasn't exactly unusual for him. They were in the back seat. He started to get angry with my mum, accused her of embarrassing him in front of his colleagues by making a joke at his expense."

I can feel the tension building in my body as his voice echoes in my ears. How can I remember it so clearly? Even now?

Lucien must sense it too because he gives my waist a gentle squeeze.

"He lunged for her," I say, my voice barely above a whisper. "I leaned back, trying to help, and the car veered off the road. We rolled into a ditch and hit a tree."

I fall silent, the memory of screeching tires and shattering glass echoing in my mind. What I don't tell him is that I blacked out. Before the car veered off the road. I was reaching for my mother and my vision blurred. Everything went hazy and black.

I comb my fingers through my hair and swallow down the lump in my throat.

Lucien doesn't push, doesn't ask for more details. Just lets me speak.

"They died." I shake my head, biting back tears. "Both of them. Because of me."

"Not because of you." Lucien's voice has changed from sympathetic to angry. He takes my chin in his hand and makes me look at him. "Do you hear me? *Not* because of you."

I nod at him, still crying.

He takes my coffee mug, and his, and moves them to the bedside table. I reach for his hand. "Lucien?"

"Yes, kitten?"

"Talking about it makes me..." My breath hitches and my hand goes to my thigh, my nails needling my skin. "I need to feel something. I need the memory to go away."

In one swift movement, he eases me back onto the bed, flips me onto my stomach, and yanks the sheets down.

"I can help with that," he says, parting my legs and positioning himself behind me. "How would you like to come?"

I wriggle back toward him.

"My hands, my mouth, or my cock?"

"Your mouth, and your fingers." I feel him settle behind me. Seconds later, his tongue is at my entrance. At first, my mind still whirrs, but as the sensations build in my core and his fingers find the spot that makes wetness flood to my pussy, the noises quiet.

Pleasure takes over.

Lucien takes over.

˜

A FEW HOURS LATER, I lie in bed, staring at the ceiling, trying to stop my mind doing somersaults. Just as he said they would, the effects of Lucien's blood are fading already. Not even twelve hours have passed and I'm starting to feel like myself again.

My body aches, a bone-deep weariness. But it has nothing to do with the *lots* of sex I had with Lucien. No, this is a familiar pain, the kind that settles in my joints and muscles when I've pushed myself too hard, when I've let my guard down.

And that's exactly what I've done.

In the moment, it was incredible. But now he's gone, locking the door behind him to go and deal with some 'urgent business', I can't help feeling like I've made a huge mistake.

I let him get close to me, let him see the cracks in my armor.

He's seen my scars, physical and emotional.

And I'm not sure I've ever felt so vulnerable.

The sex was incredible, mind-blowing, but it wasn't just physical. There was an emotional connection that I've never shared with anyone before. And the intensity is so unnerving I don't know how to handle it.

I told him about my parents, about the car crash that shattered my life. I let him see the guilt I've carried ever since. I let him see what it does to me.

I close my eyes as the memory surges up, vivid, and gut-wrenching. The screech of tires, the sickening crunch of metal, the searing pain in my legs and back and arms. The darkness. I squeeze my eyes shut tighter, trying to block it out, but it's too late.

I was trapped, upside down, the seatbelt cutting into my chest. The radio was still playing, some upbeat pop song that seemed almost funny amongst all the carnage. Blood dripped into my eyes, my hair, my mouth. I couldn't move, couldn't breathe. I thought I was going to die.

I called for my parents. I tried to look back over my shoulder, but the pain was too much, and I was pinned by something.

A tree.

Sticking through the windshield. A branch pressing down on my chest.

I called for them again but there was no answer.

I smashed the glass. Fought my way out.

A sob catches in my throat, yanking me back to the present. I curl in on myself, hugging my knees to my chest. Why did I tell Lucien about that? What was I thinking? Was I so blinded by the sex, and the way he looked at me, and the way he spoke to that werewolf?

"You don't even *think* about her. Do you understand?"

If that wasn't the hottest thing anyone has ever said to me then I don't know what is.

But even as I berate myself, I can't ignore the small, traitorous part of me that feels a connection to Lucien. He's not like the vampires who attacked me at the bookshop. He's cruel, yes, and dangerous, but there's something else there too. A flicker of humanity, buried deep.

He thinks I can't see it. But I do.

The way he wants to protect me. The way he looked at my scars.

I turn over and allow myself to scream into my pillow.

I don't even know what time of day it is. Yes, he's shown he wants to protect me. But he still has me locked up here.

And I know he's watching me. He has to be; how else would he have known I was holding a razor against my thigh?

I can't let myself get sucked in. I've been down this road before – with Steven. I thought he was different, too, thought he cared about me. But in the end, he just used me, broke me down until I was a shell of myself.

I can't let that happen again.

I can't sit here and convince myself that Lucien is capable of truly caring for me.

Look at the evidence, Luna. Just look...

He's locked you in. Locked. You. In.

Does someone do that if they care for you? If they trust you?

And he still hasn't given you answers.

I have to get out of here, and away from Lucien and his mind games. I've already tried to escape once and failed, but I can't give up. I won't. I can't stay just because the thought of never feeling him inside me again makes me feel like crying. Or because I felt safer in his arms than I ever have before. Or because his blood is the only thing in years that has muted my pain.

Gritting my teeth, I push myself out of bed, ignoring the protest of my aching muscles. I pace the room, trying to clear my head.

I need answers. I need to understand why he's doing this. Is he just another monster, playing with his food? Is it all a game? Or is there really something else going on. Something bigger.

My thoughts careen between fear and curiosity, despair and a fragile, foolish hope. I want to trust Lucien, want to believe that he's different. But I'm terrified of being wrong, and of letting myself fall into another trap.

I lean my forehead against the cool wall beside the portrait of the phoenix. There is no window now. No way out.

I'm a prisoner. And I can't let myself forget that, no matter how my treacherous heart might yearn for something more.

I have to find a way out. Even if it means leaving behind the one person who might understand my broken pieces.

CHAPTER 22
LUCIEN

The room smells of sex. Kim is at my desk, in my chair, and Trent is standing opposite practically growling.

The two of them didn't fuck. For a wolf, Trent is strangely rigid in his approach to sex; he wouldn't even contemplate being in the same room as an erect penis.

I notice the feed on the screen. Luna's room.

Kim catches me looking and adjusts his glasses. I try not to let my lip curl into a smile. So, he was watching. And it turned him on enough that he very clearly, judging from the scent in the air, got himself off to it.

Interesting.

But, right now, irrelevant.

"What's going on?" I gesture for Kim to leave my chair. He gets up and stalks around to the other side of the desk, standing next to Trent and glancing at him. "Whatever you have to say, you can say it in front of Trent." He might be a wolf, but he's a loyal wolf. Dogs are, after all, stupid.

"I went to the Crimson Moon, asked some questions."

"So, that's why you look like shit. When was the last time you slept?"

Kim looks at me with an expression that says, "Why the fuck are you asking after my sleep all of a sudden? Has Luna softened that cold, black heart?"

If we were alone, he'd make the joke out loud. But he doesn't trust Trent. According to Kim, he's a slimy mother fucker and I'm blinded by the fact he was a cute puppy once upon a time.

He might be right. But so far, Trent has given me no reason not to trust him. Except for the way he looked at Luna, and I allowed him a free pass for that.

One free pass.

"Rumor is there's a new boss in town who's trying to take over the FHB trade in the city." Kim folds his arms in front of his chest.

"I run the FHB trade." I pick up the half-drunk glass of blood on the desk and down it in one. I glance at the screen. Luna is too distracting. I shouldn't be thinking about her now. But what if this concerns her? What if it's all linked?

"Apparently, someone didn't get the memo." Kim raises his eyebrows.

"Pretty useless information unless you know who this guy is and where he's hanging out," Trent mumbles, looking smug as fuck because Kim hasn't been able to give me anything solid. He turns to me. "Let me go to the bar. I'll get some answers."

"Oh, yeah? And how will you do that?" Kim's hand moves to his belt and his fingers twitch. He carries a blade these days.

"Put your dicks away, boys. This isn't a pissing contest."

"I'll get a name." Kim looks at me and bites his lower lip. Then he says, "I need to talk to you alone, Lucien." He glances pointedly at the screen.

I hesitate. I don't like how much I trust him. He's a human. It seems unnatural to trust a human more than a super, but something tells me to listen.

"Trent. Leave us."

"Boss, seriously?" The slight whine in his voice makes me slam the glass down on the desk. He whimpers a little then mumbles, "Yes, boss. You know where I am if you need me."

When he's gone, and the door is closed, Kim leans on the desk, palms flat. "It has to be linked, right? It can't be a coincidence. A new boss trying to mustle in on the FHB trade. Someone sending vamps to attack Luna and raid her house?"

I drum my fingers on the side of the glass. On the screen, Luna is curled up in bed, sleeping.

It's daylight outside now, but with the lack of natural light in her room her body probably can't tell whether it's day or night. And she'll be coming down from the blood.

My blood.

I glance at Kim. Did he see her feeding from me? Was that what turned him on? Or was it the way I fucked her?

"Did you see what happened?" I point at the screen and Kim's complexion pales.

"Not the fucking, I know you saw that. Were you paying attention to what happened *while* we were fucking?"

He frowns at me.

I gesture for him to come and look at the screen. He stands behind my shoulder, and I skip back through the recorded footage.

I had hoped to watch this alone but needs must.

When I press play, Kim's body stiffens and the air between us thickens. "Don't watch us," I murmur. "Watch the room. Watch the shadows."

The sounds of Luna's climax fill the room.

Kim's breathing is slow and heavy.

I glance down and notice he's getting hard.

Would Luna like it if she knew? Would it make her feel proud that she's turned him on?

I wait for the usual tsunami of jealousy to rake through my body, but it doesn't come. Perhaps because Kim is so very *polite* and *respectful*, and because even though he doesn't know Luna the way I do, he cares about her safety.

Truly cares.

If he didn't, he wouldn't have been in The Crimson Moon in the middle of the night. Risking his own safety if they found out he was a hunter, and his precious six hour sleep requirement.

My gaze moves to his face now. His eyes widen, and I know what he's seen.

I skip back the feed and we watch it again.

The shadows in the corners are rippling and swirling like dark water disturbed by an unseen force. They stretch and twist, defying the laws of physics and light.

"Incredible," Kim mutters, his eyes wide.

I nod, my gaze fixed on the writhing darkness. It moves almost like a living thing, reaching tendrils towards Luna's arching form. The shadows pulse in time with her gasps, growing darker and more substantial with each wave of pleasure.

For a moment, it looks as if the entire room is engulfed in a cocoon of living shadow. Then, as Luna's climax subsides, the darkness gradually retreats, settling back into normal, motionless pools of blackness.

"I've never seen anything like it," I admit, my voice hushed.

Kim turns to me, his expression grave. "What does this mean, Lucien?"

I shake my head, still processing what we've witnessed. "I'm not sure. But whatever power Luna possesses, it's more potent than we imagined. And it's growing stronger."

"But she has no idea?"

"She didn't notice it." I skip the video back again, and again. Each time, I'm transfixed by what I'm looking at.

"Maybe it's time you told her the truth, Lucien. About the Covenant. It can't be a coincidence that her power is growing at the exact same moment a new challenger to your empire arrives in town? What if the FHB stuff is all a front? And they're really here for her?"

I hesitate, biting the inside of my cheek. I hate to admit that Kim's theory sounds plausible. But it does.

"Get me a name, Kim. Get it for me tonight."

He nods solemnly at me. "Trent?"

"No. Leave him here." I meet his eyes. "You deal with this. *You* understand we need to keep her safe."

As Kim leaves, I turn back to the screen and watch myself kissing Luna gently on the lips. Holding her close.

I am tender with her, and seeing it like this – as if I'm watching from above – is jarring.

Because in that moment, with her, I don't look like a monster. I look like a man holding a woman, trying to show her he loves her.

And *that* cannot be the truth of it.

I cannot love her.

Because if I do, I will break her.

CHAPTER 23
LUNA

I'm behind the steering wheel, my hands gripping it so tightly my knuckles are white. The road ahead is dark, illuminated only by the weak glow of my headlights and the occasional streetlamp. Snow falls in thick flurries, obscuring my vision.

The inside of the car is too warm, stuffy with the scent of alcohol and my father's expensive aftershave.

"Watch the road, Luna," my mother says, her voice tight with forced cheerfulness. "It's getting slippery out there."

I nod, not trusting myself to speak. My eyes flick to the rearview mirror. Dad's face is flushed, his eyes glassy. He's muttering under his breath, and I can see Mum's hand on his arm, trying to calm him.

"I saw the way you were looking at him," Dad suddenly growls, his words slightly slurred. "Laughing at his jokes. Making me look like a fool."

"Darling, please," Mum whispers. "Not now. Luna's driving."

But he's not listening. His voice rises, filling the car. "You think I didn't notice? You think I'm stupid?"

I grip the wheel tighter, trying to focus on the road. The car feels like it's sliding slightly, and I ease off the accelerator.

"Dad," I say, my voice trembling. "Maybe we should pull over?"

He ignores me completely. "Answer me!" he shouts at my mother. "Were you flirting with him? Planning to leave me for that smug bastard?"

"Of course not," she says, her voice cracking. "You're being ridiculous. You've had too much to drink."

I see his hand raise in the mirror, and my heart leaps into my throat. "Dad, no!" I cry out, turning in my seat.

Everything happens in slow motion. Dad's hand comes down, but Mum flinches away. He lunges for her, and she presses herself against the car door. I reach back, trying to intervene, my eyes leaving the road.

That's when I feel it. The car hits a patch of black ice, and suddenly we're spinning. The world outside the windows becomes a dizzying blur of white snow and dark trees. I hear Mum scream, feel Dad's hand grasp my shoulder hard enough to bruise.

I turn back to the front, yanking the wheel desperately, but it's too late. We're sliding off the road, picking up speed as we roll into a ditch. Through the windshield, I see the massive trunk of a pine tree rushing towards us.

The impact is deafening. Metal crunches, glass shatters. My body jerks forward, then slams back into the seat. Pain explodes everywhere at once. Something warm and wet trickles down my face.

For a moment, everything is silent except for the hiss of steam rising from the crumpled hood. Then I hear it – a low, pained moan from the back seat.

"Mum?" I croak, my voice barely a whisper. "Dad?"

No response. Just that awful moaning.

I try to turn, to look back, but I'm suspended upside down and a sharp pain is lancing through my neck and back. My legs feel strange — heavy and yet somehow not there at all. Panic rises in my throat.

"Help," I call out weakly. "Someone help us!"

But we're alone. No one is coming.

The smell of petrol fills the air, mixing with the metallic scent of blood. Somewhere in the distance, I hear sirens. Or is that just the ringing in my ears?

I blink, and suddenly I'm outside the car. How did I get here? I'm lying on the cold ground, staring up at the sky. Snowflakes fall on my face, melting instantly. They should feel cold, but I can't feel anything.

Shadows move around me. Voices shout, but they sound far away, underwater. Blue lights flash, painting the ground in strange colors.

"We've got a live one here!" someone yells. A face appears above me, a man in a paramedic's uniform. "Can you hear me, miss? What's your name?"

I try to speak, but no words come out. My eyes drift past him, to the mangled wreck of our car. I can see a still form being pulled from the back seat.

No. No, no, no.

The paramedic is speaking again, but his words fade into a dull roar. Darkness creeps in at the edges of my vision. I try to fight it, but it's too strong.

As consciousness slips away, one thought echoes in my mind: this is all my fault.

I jolt awake, my heart pounding so hard I can feel it in my throat. The room is pitch black, and for a moment, I'm back in the car, trapped in the wreckage. Panic claws at my chest, stealing my breath.

"No, no, no," I gasp, my hands flailing out, searching for something, anything to ground me.

They connect with something solid and warm. Lucien. He's here, kneeling on the bed beside me. The realization should calm me, but instead, it amplifies my panic. I'm trapped. Locked in. Caged.

"Luna?" His voice is thick with concern, but all I can hear is the crunch of metal, the shattering of glass.

"Let me out!" I cry, my fists connecting with his chest. "I can't be here. I can't be locked in anymore. I can't!"

My voice rises to a shriek as I pummel him. I need to get out, need to breathe, need to escape.

Lucien doesn't try to stop me or restrain my flailing arms. Instead, he scoops me up. I feel the rush of air as he moves at inhuman speed, and suddenly we're in the hallway.

"Let me go!" I demand, still fighting against his hold. "Put me down!"

He doesn't respond, just tightens his grip and keeps moving. We're going downstairs now, my stomach lurching with each rapid descent. I squeeze my eyes shut, torn between the claustrophobia of being held and the fear of being dropped.

And then, abruptly, we stop. Cold air hits my skin, and I gasp. My eyes fly open.

We're outside.

I'm wearing nothing but a t-shirt and a pair of black underwear, and it's the middle of winter. Goosebumps slither over my flesh.

The panic recedes slightly as I gulp in the crisp night air. Stars twinkle overhead, so bright and clear it takes my breath away. I've never seen them like this in the city.

Lucien is still holding me. I become acutely aware of my state of undress, but the cool air feels good against my overheated skin.

"Better?" Lucien asks softly, his breath warm against my ear.

I nod, not trusting my voice just yet. My heart is still racing, but the blind panic has subsided.

He starts moving again, this time at a normal pace. We descend a series of stone steps, winding through a beautifully landscaped garden. In the moonlight, I can make out the shapes of sculpted hedges and delicate flowers.

The path ends at what looks like a large, steaming swimming pool. The water's surface ripples gently, sending tendrils of mist curling into the night air.

Lucien sets me down gently at the top of the pool steps. "Get in," he says.

I hesitate, wrapping my arms around myself. "I don't have a swimsuit."

A small smile plays at the corners of his mouth. "You don't need one. Just get in."

Part of me wants to refuse. But I can feel the residual panic still thrumming through my veins and the thought of being in the water, being lighter and cocooned by something smooth and warm and beautiful, draws me in.

Taking a deep breath, I step into the pool. The water is deliciously warm. I wade in deeper, my underwear and my t-shirt soaking up the water.

When I'm waist deep, I turn back to look at Lucien. He's standing at the edge of the pool, watching me intently. In the moonlight, the red flecks in his eyes are more visible. Yet, in this moment, I've never felt safer.

I wade out further until the water reaches my shoulders, then lean back, letting myself float. The water cradles me effortlessly. Above me, the stars shine brilliantly in the vast expanse of sky.

For the first time in what feels like forever, I feel like I can breathe freely. The nightmare, the memories, the pain - they're still there, but they feel less immediate, less overwhelming.

I close my eyes, focusing on the sensations around me. The gentle lapping of water against my skin. The cool breeze on my face. The distant rustle of leaves in the garden.

When I open my eyes again, Lucien is sitting at the edge of the pool, shoes beside him, bare feet dangling in the water. He's watching me with an expression I can't quite decipher — part concern, part fascination.

"Thank you," I say softly, moving toward him.

"You're welcome, Luna."

"Come and join me?"

"I don't swim."

"Lucien. Come and join me." I address him more forcefully now.

He raises an eyebrow at me. Something inside him both resents me and adores me when I talk to him like this; I can see it in his eyes.

Slowly, he stands up and slips off his shirt.

"Pants, too," I tell him.

He rolls his tongue over his fangs and smirks at me.

"Boxers." I bite my lower lip as he rolls them over his hips, exposing his cock. In return, I peel off my wet t-shirt then reach beneath the water and take off my panties, too.

Lucien flexes his shoulders, then stands at the edge of the pool and dives in. He disappears underwater, moving like an Olympic swimmer, and appears again at the other end of the pool. He flicks his wet hair from his eyes then swims toward me.

"I thought you said you don't swim?"

"I should have said I don't *like* to swim."

I loop my arms around his neck and my legs around his waist. I can feel his cock at my entrance. Without any lead up, I slide down onto him and gasp as he fills me. He groans loudly and his eyes flash with pleasure.

But then he brushes my damp hair from my face. "Are you all right?"

I continue staring into his eyes. "It was a nightmare."

"Your parents?"

I nuzzle into his neck and focus on moving up and down on his shaft, pleasure slowly building. "I don't want to talk about it."

"What do you want to talk about?" His breath hitches as I tilt my hips. He kisses my throat. His teeth graze my skin but do not break it, and I realize that a part of me wants him to.

I comb my fingers through his wet hair.

"Tell me the truth, Lucien. Tell me why you're keeping me here."

"Luna..."

"If you want me to trust you, you have to tell me the truth."

There is a pause. Lucien has stopped moving. He takes his hands from my waist and then he's gone. He's no longer inside me. "Why would I care if you trust me?"

His tone is hard and dark. His eyes are dark, too.

"Because we..."

"What?" He swims to the edge of the pool and levers himself out of it, grabbing his clothes, cock still hard. When he turns to face me, he meets my eyes. "Because we fucked?"

He holds my gaze defiantly, daring me to challenge him and to say out loud that it was more than just fucking.

"You can tell me what to do when we're in bed," he growls. "But you don't tell me how to run my business. You let me handle it. Understand?"

His tone sends shivers through me. Not the good kind. It reminds me of Steven, and my father, and suddenly I have no words. My strength is gone. My voice is stuck in my throat, and I feel like I want to cry and run and hide all at the same time.

"Do you understand?"

The last time he asked me that question, it was with tenderness. This time, he sounds vicious. He sounds like *them*.

I lower my gaze. I can't look at him.

"Time to go back inside." He strides to a small structure that looks like a pool house and returns seconds later with a towel. He stands at the top of the steps and holds it out for me.

Disappointment, embarrassment, and hurt hum on my skin.

As Lucien watches me, his whole body stiffens. He hands me the towel but does not wrap it around me or kiss me. Then he turns and marches back toward the house.

And I follow him. Because what else can I do?

CHAPTER 24
LUCIEN

I take her back to her room and close the door without saying another word. I can't look at her. Because the way she looked at me almost ended me.

She thinks I'm like them. The men who hurt her. In that one moment, by speaking to her as if she was nothing to me, I broke the trust she had in me. And I broke her.

Not the way they did.

But enough.

And I hate myself for it.

She believes love equals control, and that she can't trust a lover to keep her safe. I was trying to prove her wrong, but I'm a monster. Of course, I can't give her what she needs.

I don't deserve her. I should have stayed away, kept watching her in the shadows. I should never have allowed myself the privilege of getting close to her.

Back in my study, I deliberately do not turn on the camera feed to her bedroom.

I can't watch her crying.

My heart swells in my chest. What if she...? I think of the razor in her hand. Would she? Now that the trust between us is broken?

I slam my fist into the wall so hard it makes the plaster crumble. My knuckles bleed but heal quickly. I punch it again, and again, and again, watching my skin break and heal, break and heal.

The thought of losing her is unbearable and, yet, I never really had her. It was all make believe.

I pace the length of my study. My hands clench and unclench at my sides, fighting the urge to tear the entire room to pieces, to unleash the storm of emotions raging inside me.

How could I have been so foolish? To think that I, a creature of darkness and blood, could offer Luna anything but pain and disappointment. I've lived for centuries, and all I have ever brought to this world is destruction and pain. What made me believe I could be different for her?

The memory of her face, the hurt and fear in her eyes, haunts me. I've seen that look before, on countless victims throughout the years. But it has never cut me so deeply.

I stop at the window and pull back the shutters so I can stare out into the night. The darkness that once felt like home now seems oppressive, a reflection of the void inside me. Luna deserves light, warmth, safety - all the things I can never truly provide.

My reflection mocks me, reminding me of who I really am, and of what I've done. The countless lives I've taken, the joy I once found in cruelty - it's all part of me. A part I can never fully escape, no matter how much I might wish to. No matter how much she made me feel... different.

I've been playing at being human, at being worthy of her trust and affection. But it has all been a lie. A beautiful, intoxicating lie that I allowed myself to believe.

No more.

I pick up my phone and text Trent. *Have a blood donor brought up here as soon as possible. Young. Male. B+ blood type.*

Immediately, Trent replies. *Yes, boss. Anything else?*

I don't answer him.

I am already thinking about sinking my teeth into the throat of whoever arrives on the doorstep.

The truth is, I'm at my best when I embrace what I am. Ruthless. Efficient. Alone. These are the qualities that have kept me alive for centuries, that have made me feared and respected. Not just in this city but in every place I've ever lived.

These are the qualities that allowed me to rise up to take control of this place. And these are the tools I need to use now, to keep Luna safe and to figure out what she is.

Because that's what this has to be about now. Not my selfish desires, not my misguided attempt at redemption through her love. She's in danger - from the Covenant, from rival vampires, from forces I don't yet understand. And the only way I can truly protect her is by treating her like a job.

The way I treated her when I very first set eyes on her all those years ago.

No more tender moments. No more pretending. I need to be cold, calculated. I need to be the monster I've always been, and I need to channel it into keeping her safe.

Then, when it's over, and when the threat is neutralized, I'll set her free. I'll give her the chance at a normal life, at finding love with someone worthy of her light. Someone human, unbroken, unburdened by centuries of darkness.

The decision settles over me like a shroud. It hurts - more than I thought possible - but it feels right. This is who I am. This is what I do. I'm not meant for love or happiness. I'm a predator without a soul. And it's time I remembered that.

CHAPTER 25
KIM

The abandoned warehouse looms before me, its broken windows like hollow eyes staring out into the night.

Why is it always an abandoned warehouse? Never a fancy hotel or a nice plush bar in the center of town?

The stench of decay and something sickeningly sweet hangs in the air. Fermented Human Blood. FHB.

I've never tried the stuff, but I've seen what it does to both vampires and humans. At least when the queen was alive, everything was pretty well regulated. Since Lucien killed her, the FHB problem has been getting worse. And I can't help feeling like whoever is trying to take over is using it as a distraction.

I think back to the video feed, trying not to think too much about the image of Luna and Lucien fucking. Instead, I think about the shadows.

She had no idea what she was doing. But it was like she was calling them to her.

If someone else suspects her power, then they'll have been

watching her. Which means they will know Lucien watches her, too.

Perhaps they're causing chaos in the city to keep him distracted.

I bite my lower lip. For the first time, maybe ever, I wish Trent was here just so I had someone to talk this shit through with out loud. Lucien's so caught up in having her in the mansion, close to him, he's not really interested in exploring theories. He wants facts. A name.

So, that's what I'm here to find.

I adjust my grip on the stake in my jacket pocket, taking a deep breath. Coming here as a human is beyond risky, but a nest of FHB laced vamps with little control over what they say is my best shot at getting information on the new boss in town.

Slipping through a gap in the chain-link fence, I make my way toward the building. The closer I get, the stronger the smell becomes. It's cloying, almost dizzying. I can't imagine what it does to a vampire's heightened senses.

I flex my fingers on the stake. The dark energy swirling around this place is suffocating. Everything inside me tells me to run. But, as usual, I ignore that instinct and head straight for danger.

Inside, the warehouse is a maze of rusted machinery and crumbling walls. I strain my ears for any sound of movement.

There – a soft moan from the far end of the building.

I creep forward, trying not to make a sound. As I round a corner, I see them. A group of vampires, maybe six or seven, sprawled across dirty mattresses and broken furniture. Their skin is pale, almost translucent, with black veins spider-webbing across their faces. Their eyes, when they flutter open, are completely black.

FHB users. And by the looks of it, they're deep in the throes of addiction.

I scan the group, looking for my target. I need a baby vamp, someone more pliable than the others. They're easy to spot; their energy is different. More erratic, animalistic, unpredictable. Which, though dangerous, is what I need.

A young man, probably a university student, sits up, swaying slightly, his gaze unfocused. Perfect.

Taking a deep breath, I step into view. "Hey," I call out softly. "You okay, man?"

The young vampire's head snaps up, his black eyes fixing on me. For a moment, there's no recognition, no hint of humanity. Then he blinks, and something like awareness flickers in his gaze.

"Who... who are you?" His voice is raspy, barely above a whisper.

I move closer, hands raised to show I'm not a threat. "Name's Kim. I'm looking for someone. Thought you might be able to help."

He laughs, a hollow, brittle sound. "Me? Help? I can't even help myself."

I crouch down beside him, keeping one eye on the other vampires. They seem too far gone to be a threat, but if they smell a human, that might change.

"I'm looking for the new boss in town. The one supplying this stuff." I gesture at the empty vials scattered around.

The vampire tenses, fear flashing across his face. "I don't know anything about that."

"Come on, man," I press, injecting a note of desperation into my voice. "I need some good stuff. My supplier disappeared, and I'm hurting. Just need to know who to talk to."

The vampire's eyes narrow, a flicker of suspicion cutting through his drug-addled haze. "But you're human," he says, his voice a low growl.

I shrug. "Humans can handle FHB too, you know. It's not just for vamps. The high is... something else."

He seems to consider this, his black eyes roving over me. I can see the wheels turning in his hazy brain, weighing the risk of trusting me against the possibility of gaining a new customer for his boss.

"Look," I say, glancing nervously at the other stirring vampires. "Can we talk outside? I'm not comfortable with all these... others around. Don't want them taking a cut of your commission if you're the one to introduce me. You know?"

After a moment's hesitation, he nods and a smile spreads across his face. "Yeah... yeah, okay. We gotta stick together, don't we? Us younger guys." He glances at the other vampires, who are honestly impossible to age. Then sticks out his hand and lets me help him up.

We make our way out of the warehouse, the vampire stumbling slightly. Once outside, I lead him around to a secluded spot behind the building.

"So," he says, rolling up his sleeves. "How much quantity are we talking about. You have others who want in?"

He's still speaking when I pin him against the wall, my stake pressed firmly against his chest.

"What the—" he grumbles, straining against me.

He's strong, but I'm pressing the stake down right above his heart and any moment at all could cause me to puncture his chest.

"Who's the new boss? Who's supplying the FHB?"

"I said I'd get you some. There's no need for—"

"I don't need product. I need a name."

The vampire frowns at me. Then shakes his head. "I don't know what you're talking about," he gasps, struggling against my grip.

I press the stake harder, feeling it bite into his flesh. "Wrong answer. Last chance. Who's running things now?"

Terror floods his face. "I can't... they'll kill me if I talk."

"I'll kill you if you don't," I counter.

Something in my voice must convince him because he slumps in defeat. "Fuck," he mutters. Then, "Nix," he whispers. "That's the name I've heard. Nix."

"Nix?"

He nods. "I swear. That's all I know. Just the name."

"Thank you," I say quietly. Then, before he can react, I drive the stake through his heart and his body crumbles to dust. Then I take out my phone and dial Lucien.

"Kim?"

"Does the name *Nix* mean anything to you?"

There is silence on the end of the phone. All I can hear is Lucien's breathing. When he speaks, his voice sounds different.

"Nix?" he mutters.

Dread solidifies in my stomach. Because, for the first time, Lucien Thornfield sounds scared.

CHAPTER 26
LUCIEN
ENGLAND, 1645

The scent of fear hangs thick in the air as Nix and I approach the village. Moonlight glints off the thatched roofs, and smoke curls from chimneys. It's a peaceful scene, soon to be shattered.

"Ready, brother?" Nix grins at me, his fangs gleaming in the darkness.

I nod, feeling the familiar rush of anticipation. "Always."

We move silently through the shadows, two predators on the hunt. The first house is easy — a simple wooden latch that I break with a flick of my wrist. Inside, a family sleeps, unaware of the monsters at their door.

Nix takes the parents, his hand clamped over the mother's mouth to muffle her screams. I go for the children, draining them quickly. Their blood is intoxicatingly sweet; innocence tinged with terror.

As we emerge, faces smeared with blood, I feel alive. Powerful. Unstoppable.

"Next one?" Nix asks, his eyes wild with bloodlust.

We tear through the village like a storm, leaving death and destruction in our wake. Screams fill the night air, a symphony of terror that only fuels our frenzy.

In one house, we find a young woman hiding in a closet. Nix pulls her out, her terrified whimpers music to our ears.

"This one's pretty," he says, running a finger down her tear-stained cheek. "Shall we keep her?"

I consider it for a moment, then shake my head. "No loose ends, brother. You know the rules."

Nix pouts playfully but doesn't argue. He sinks his fangs into her neck, and I watch as the life drains from her eyes.

We move on, house after house falling to our insatiable hunger. Some try to fight, others to flee. It makes no difference. We are death incarnate, and none can escape us.

We are the most powerful beings in existence.

Our father told us so.

In the village square, we face a group of men armed with pitchforks and torches. It's almost laughable how outmatched they are.

"Shall we play with them a bit?" Nix suggests, a cruel smile twisting his features.

I nod, matching his grin. "Why not? We have all night."

What follows is a game of cat and mouse, toying with the villagers as they try desperately to defend their homes and families. We're too fast, too strong. Their weapons are useless against us.

A burly man swings his pitchfork at me. I catch it easily, wrenching it from his grasp and impaling him on his own weapon. His shocked expression as he falls is oddly satisfying.

Nix, meanwhile, is toying with three younger men. He darts between them, slashing with his sharp fingernails, drawing out their pain and fear. "Come now," he taunts, "surely you can do better than this?"

One of the men, braver or more foolish than the rest, charges at Nix with a torch. My brother sidesteps easily, grabbing the man's arm and using his momentum to send him crashing into his companions. In the blink of an eye, Nix is on them, fangs tearing into flesh.

As the night wears on, our game becomes more elaborate, more cruel. We chase a group of survivors into the church, listening to their desperate prayers with amusement.

"Shall we show them how powerless their god is?" I suggest, eyeing the heavy wooden doors.

Nix's eyes light up. "Oh yes, let's. Father would so enjoy hearing about it."

Together, we rip the doors from their hinges. The screams from inside reach a fevered pitch as we enter this supposed sanctuary.

"Your god can't save you," I announce, my voice echoing in the vaulted space. "We are your deities now."

What follows is a massacre. Blood stains the stone floor, seeping into the cracks. We desecrate the altar, turning their place of worship into a tomb.

As dawn approaches, we stand amidst the carnage. The village is silent now, save for the crackling of fires and the occasional moan of a survivor we've left to suffer.

Nix claps me on the shoulder, his laughter echoing in the empty square. "Now that, brother, was a feast!"

I survey the destruction, feeling a sense of pride and power. This is what it means to be a vampire — to take what we want, to revel in our superiority over these fragile humans.

"Indeed it was," I agree, wiping blood from my chin. "Though I fear we may have been a touch... overzealous."

Nix raises an eyebrow. "Oh? Having regrets, Lucien?"

I shake my head. "Not regrets. But this level of destruction... it will be noticed. We'll need to lay low for a while."

My brother scoffs. "Let them come. We'll give them the same treatment."

As we leave the ruined village behind, I feel no remorse, no guilt. Only satisfaction and a hunger for more.

The world is ours for the taking, and we will paint it red with the blood of humans.

I glance at Nix, seeing my own bloodlust reflected in his eyes. "Where to next, brother?"

CHAPTER 27
LUNA

I stand under the shower for a long time. Floating in Lucien's swimming pool, and the way he carried me outside holding me close, feels like a distant memory already. And I can't connect it to the way he looked at me when he told me to stay out of his *business*.

How did I allow myself to forget what he was?

I fell into the same trap I have always fallen into; trusting someone who has literally shown me exactly what they are right from the beginning.

Choosing to believe that this time it will be different.

Lucien *murdered* someone and sent me their body parts. He is a vampire. He drinks human blood. And on top of that, he's some kind of supernatural gangster. He *ate* another vampire's heart.

But still, I let the heat in his gaze distract me. I believed his touch, and the softness in his eyes, and the things he made my body feel instead of the facts.

I believed he was falling for me, and I thought I was falling for him too. I thought this was what it felt like to finally be safe.

I was wrong.

I am not safe with him, and I never will be. So, it's time to stop pretending. It is time to leave this place.

I pull on my clothes and pace the room. I tug at the painting Kim hung back over the window, and take it down. I try prying my fingers beneath the sheet of MDF, but there is no gap and it is held firmly in place by the nails Kim hammered into the wall.

I examine every crevice, searching both for a way out and for the camera I know he uses to watch me. I find it in the eye of a statue. A skull with a caved in head that holds a clutch of black roses. I turn it to face the wall.

No more watching.

No more.

My heartbeat quickens. My ribs feel tight, like my breath is swelling against them and threatening to crack them in two. The lights flicker. For a moment, I think Lucien is doing it to mess with me but then they right themselves.

I cross to the door and try the handle. It is locked. I am about to turn away when I hear footsteps outside.

My stomach clenches.

Has he come back?

Why the fuck do I feel relieved? excited to see him instead of dreading it. Hopeful that he might have changed his mind and come to apologize; to show me he's sorry and that he knows he was wrong. To do what my father and Steven never did and admit his failings.

I hear a key in the lock. It turns and clicks. I stand back, waiting for the door to open. But it doesn't.

A long moment passes and still Lucien doesn't appear.

So, I try the handle again myself. I push. And the door opens.

The corridor is almost pitch dark, lit by just a few muted wall lights. Hard floor, long red rug running down the center. The same eerie paintings and pictures.

I stare into the shadows. But there is no one there.

Immediately, my thoughts go to Kim. *If things change, I'll let you know.*

Is he setting me free? Telling me to run?

My feet are bare, but there is no time to go back inside and fetch socks and shoes. If I'm going, I have to go now.

I let the door close behind me and move quickly down the hall. Down the same stairs Lucien carried me when he took me outside, through the entrance hall, out of the large wooden doors and onto the steps in front of the house.

Then I run.

Down the driveway between two lines of silver birch trees, standing like sentinels watching over me, toward the large wrought iron gates that separate Lucien's estate from the outside world.

I have no idea how I'm going to get out. All I know is I have to try.

I am a few feet away when I hear the dogs. I look back over my shoulder and then my foot catches on something sharp. It's bleeding but I don't stop. I keep running.

I reach the gates and wrap my fingers around the cold metal, puling as hard as I can. Rattling them frantically as my heart hammer and my lungs swell and my body screams with desperation.

I try to climb but there is nothing to hold onto.

I move to the wall and try there. I manage to find a foot hold but it's not enough.

The dogs are louder now. Closer.

Above, thunder cracks and seconds later a fork of lightning

illuminates the night sky. It has been weeks since we had rain. Of course, it would choose to arrive tonight.

I return to the gates. I lift my arms higher so they're straining, and my shoulders hurt and use every ounce of strength I possess to pull myself up high enough so that I can slot my feet onto the metal bar that sits a couple of feet above the ground. There is another to my right. Too far out of reach to be easy, but I have no other option.

This. This is why I should have tried harder in gym classes at school. *This* is why I hate my body; I always knew I wouldn't survive a zombie apocalypse, but it didn't occur to me that being able to escape vampires was a necessary skill.

I have just managed to move my feet to the next metal bar when it starts to rain. The gates become instantly slick and slippery. My bare feet struggle to keep hold, and my fingers can't get enough purchase to pull me up any higher.

I am stuck.

I look down at the ground. It is not a big jump. Maybe five feet. But just when I'm contemplating letting myself drop, they appear as if from nowhere – the dogs. Four of them.

They gather at the bottom of the gate, jaws snapping, barking, shining black fur wet from the rain. A fifth appears. Different from the rest. Grey with bright blue eyes.

Why does that dog look familiar?

I turn away and try to adjust my grasp on the gate. I have to keep going. I can't go back. But the second I reach for the next metal bar, I lose my hold.

And I fall.

My body meets the ground with a force that knocks the breath clean out of my chest. Rain pummels my face. Pain ricochets through me, scraping down my bones, clawing my insides, making my muscles constrict and twist and throb.

I try to move and realize my shoulder is sticking out at a strange angle. Panic rises in my stomach. My vision blurs. Everything is going black. Like it did when I was sitting in my upturned car with my parents' dead bodies.

The sound of the car radio echoes in my ears. I hear glass breaking, and my parents screaming, and the darkness keeps closing in.

"Do you need a hand?"

I open my eyes. The dogs are quiet, and Trent – Lucien's security guard – is standing above me smiling.

I blink up at him and I'm about to cry with gratitude when I realize his eyes are bright blue. Like the dog's.

I turn my head. Now there are only four.

I look back at him. "You're a werewolf?"

He nods and folds his arms in front of his chest. "You're injured," he says, nodding at my shoulder. "You really shouldn't have tried to escape."

I try to scramble back, away from him, but he clicks his fingers at the dogs, and they crowd together behind me. "Did you unlock my door?"

Trent tilts his head. "Why would I do that?"

"So, you could be the one to rescue me?" Fury flares in my gut. Is he that desperate for Lucien's approval? Is he that pathetic?

With a dry laugh, Trent sweeps some rain from his eyes and shakes his head. "I didn't let you go so I could rescue you, Luna." He licks his lips.

My bare feet are now covered in mud. My body screams in pain. My shoulder... my shoulder.

"I let you go so I could chase you."

CHAPTER 28
LUCIEN

I slam her bedroom door open, expecting resistance. But it wasn't locked. Who the fuck unlocked it?

I stride in, searching for her, almost blind with panic at the thought of her being gone. Being out of reach.

The room is empty. She has turned the camera away, so it's facing the wall. She no longer wanted me to see her.

Her shoes are by the bed.

Where is she?

I tear through the room at superhuman speed, ripping the paintings from the walls and the sheets from the bed as though I might find her hiding from me.

I can barely breathe.

Did I forget to lock her in? Has she run?

I let out a loud roar and lift the armchair, then throw it at the wall. I am leaning onto my knees, breathing hard, trying to sense her scent in the air, when something shifts.

The temperature changes. It becomes instantly cooler. When I look up again, the shadows are moving.

They dance across the wall, morphing into distinct shapes. My breath catches in my throat as I watch the silhouettes form a familiar figure – Luna. Her shadow-self runs, long hair streaming behind her. She reaches the gates and tries to climb.

The dogs are chasing her but then there is another figure.

Larger, more menacing. A wolf. Its jaws are open, teeth bared, gaining on her with each loping stride.

"Trent," I whisper, white hot rage pooling behind my eyes.

The shadows shift again, showing Luna trying to climb the gate. Losing her footing. Falling.

She is on the ground now, writhing in pain, and Trent is moving toward her.

Suddenly, the room plunges into complete darkness. The shadows have swallowed every bit of light, leaving me in a void so absolute I can hardly breathe.

Then, as quickly as it came, the darkness recedes. The shadows pull back to the corners of the room, leaving me standing in the wreckage of my panic.

My mind races. Is this Luna's power? Is she calling for me?

It doesn't matter; she is in danger, and I need to find her. Now.

I close my eyes, forcing myself to focus. To think. Where would she go? How far could she have gotten?

I'm out the door and down the stairs in a heartbeat, moving faster than any human eye could follow. The cool night air hits my face as I burst out of the mansion, rain pelting my skin. I scan the tree-lined driveway, searching desperately.

There — a scream pierces the night, coming from the direction of the gates. I push myself harder, my feet barely touching the muddy ground as I race towards the sound.

I round the last bend and the scene before me makes my blood run cold. Luna is lying on the ground, her body soaked and shivering. Her arm is jutting out unnaturally and the dogs – my dogs – are gathered behind her giving her no way to escape.

Towering over her, snarling, is Trent.

Without hesitation, I launch myself at him. We collide just as his hand reaches for Luna, the impact sending us rolling across the wet grass in a tangle of limbs and snapping jaws. Trent is strong, but I'm stronger. And far, far angrier.

With a roar of rage, I grab Trent by the throat, lifting him off the ground. His eyes widen in shock and fear as he realizes his mistake. "Lucien," he chokes out, "I can explain. It was a game. I wouldn't have hurt her. I wouldn't have—"

I don't give him the chance. With one swift motion, I snap his neck. The sound echoes in the rainy night, followed by the dull thud of his body hitting the ground.

I stare down at him as the rain batters his pale face. "I never should have trusted a wolf," I spit, barely able to control the rage coursing through me. I want to destroy his corpse. Rip his limbs free and feed them to the dogs.

"Lucien…" Luna's voice makes me turn around.

Panting, I run to her. She's shaking, rain streaming down her face. "Lucien," she whispers, her voice trembling.

I move towards her, wanting nothing more than to take her in my arms, to assure myself that she's real, that she's safe. But before I can reach her, the shadows around us begin to writhe and twist.

They surge up from the ground, from the trees, from the very air itself. They swirl around Luna, caressing her skin like dark flames. Her eyes widen in a mix of fear and wonder as the shadows respond to her presence.

As I watch, stunned, the shadows form a protective cocoon around her, shielding her from the rain. And from me.

And in that moment, I know I was right.

"Do you trust me?" I ask her.

She sits up, tears merging with the rain. "I don't know."

"Look at me, Luna." I meet her gaze. "Do you trust me?"

As her resolve to hate me weakens, the shadows dissolve and I reach for her. I skim my hands down her body. She smells of blood. Something is bleeding.

"My shoulder."

"It's dislocated. I need to pop it back in."

Her eyes spring wider and she shakes her head.

"It will hurt. But I have to."

I gently place my hands on her shoulders, feeling the unnatural angle of the joint. Luna's face is pale, her breathing shallow with pain and fear.

"Look at me," I say softly, catching her gaze. "It will be quick. I promise."

She nods, her lower lip trembling. I can hear her heart racing, smell the adrenaline coursing through her veins.

"On three," I say, positioning my hands. "One..."

In a flash, before I even say "two," I move. My speed and strength allow me to rotate and push the joint back into place with precise force. There's a sickening pop, followed immediately by Luna's sharp cry of pain.

The entire process takes less than a second.

Luna gasps, her good hand flying to her newly relocated shoulder. Tears spring to her eyes, but the relief is evident on her face as the intense pain gives way to a duller ache.

"You said on three," she manages to say, her voice shaky but with a hint of reproach.

I give her a small, apologetic smile. "It's better when you don't expect it. The tension makes it worse."

"I knew I shouldn't have trusted you."

My gut twists, but then she smiles at me. Gently, I run my

hand over her shoulder, checking to make sure everything is in place. "How does it feel?"

"Sore," she admits, blinking at me through the rain, "but better. Thank you."

I nod, then pull her close, careful not to jostle her injured arm. "Let's get you inside and dry."

As I scoop her into my arms, I can't shake the image of the shadows protecting her. Whatever's happening, whatever she is becoming, she has no idea how powerful she is. And I'm not sure I do either.

CHAPTER 29
KIM

Thornfield hung up without saying another word.

Whoever Nix is, Thornfield knows him; that much is obvious. And he's scared of him. Which, frankly, terrifies the living shit out of me because Thornfield isn't scared of anything.

Ever.

I'm contemplating whether to go back to the mansion when one of the other FHB vampires stumbles out of the warehouse. As he staggers toward the hole in the chain link fence, my instincts tell me to follow.

I fucking hate my instincts sometimes.

Twenty minutes later, I'm crouched behind a crumbling tombstone in an abandoned churchyard. We are on the outskirts of the city, not too far from Lucien's mansion.

The vampire I followed joins a gathered crowd. There must be thirty or forty of them – a mix of vampires and werewolves, which is a strange alliance because vamps and wolves historically *do not* get along. It's why I always thought Thornfield's loyalty to Trent was misplaced.

The air thrums with tension and darkness. Thunder rumbles in the sky and thick drops of rain begin to fall.

The energy is almost chokingly thick. My entire body fizzes with it, like seasickness, making it hard to focus.

My stake is in one hand, my blade in the other. But, honestly, if I'm discovered I don't stand a chance of getting out of here alive.

Clearly, this is not an event meant for human eyes or ears.

As I watch, a figure emerges from the shadows of the dilapidated church, and the crowd falls silent. Even from this distance, I can feel the power radiating off him. This must be Nix.

A vampire.

He's tall, easily over six feet. His dark blond hair is slicked back, and he has sharp, aristocratic features that give him an air of nobility.

When he smiles at his audience, there's a cruel twist to his lips that sends a chill down my spine. He seems not to even notice the rain.

In slightly cliched fashion, his long black coat billows slightly in the breeze, revealing black jeans and a fitted black shirt underneath. He positions himself at the front of the church and clicks his fingers.

A massive black dog appears at his side, its thick jaw and pointed ears giving it an almost demonic appearance. It sits beside him and licks its lips.

Then Nix raises his hands. When he speaks, his voice carries easily across the graveyard. It's a rich, cultured voice, tinged with an accent I can't quite place - something old. Something that makes my skin prickle and my breath thicken in my lungs.

"My friends," he begins, his tone smooth and charismatic. "We stand on the precipice of a new era. For too long, we've hidden in the shadows, scraping by on the fringes of society. But no more!"

Hidden in the shadows? Supers have been out in the open for years now...

But a murmur of agreement ripples through the crowd.

"Look around you," Nix continues, pacing before his rapt audience. His movements are fluid, almost hypnotic. "Vampires and werewolves, age-old enemies, standing together. This is just the beginning of what we can achieve when we unite under a common cause."

He pauses, his gaze sweeping over the gathered supernatural creatures. Lightning forks in the sky, illuminating the graveyard. "For centuries, humans have ruled this world. They've hunted us, feared us, tried to destroy us. And why? Because they outnumber us? Because they control the daylight hours?" He scoffs, a sound filled with derision. "No. They rule because we have allowed it."

The crowd shifts restlessly, a mix of excitement and apprehension in the air.

"They have forced us to mold ourselves in their image. Integrate into *their* society. Live by *their* rules. But why? We are stronger. We are more powerful. We are superior."

A cheer ripples through the watching supers.

"We should be the ones dictating the rules. Not them!"

Another cheer.

"But Cambridge is just the beginning," Nix declares, his volume rising. "We will take control not just of this city, but of *every* city. We will step out of the shadows and take our rightful place as the apex predators of this world!"

I grip my weapons tighter, my heart racing.

Nix waits for the noise to die down before continuing. "Imagine a world where we don't have to hide what we are. Where we can hunt freely, where our power is acknowledged and respected. A world where we make the rules, and humans are nothing more than cattle to serve our needs."

He's painting a vivid picture, and I can see the crowd getting caught up in his vision. It's terrifying how persuasive he is.

"But this isn't just about dominance," Nix says, his voice softening. "It's about freedom. Freedom to be who we truly are, without fear or shame. Freedom to build a society that caters to our needs, our desires. A world where we can thrive, not just survive."

A voice calls out from the crowd, "How? How can we possibly do that? The humans outnumber us, and they have weapons, technology..."

Nix smiles, a predatory grin that sends a shiver down my spine. He pauses for dramatic effect, his eyes scanning the crowd. When he speaks again, his voice is low, almost reverent.

"What if I told you there was an ancient power that could turn the tide in our favor? A power that could bend reality itself to our will?"

The audience falls silent, hanging on his every word.

Nix rests his palm on his dog's head and strokes its ears. Then he looks up and says, "Who here has heard of The Covenant of Shadows?"

CHAPTER 30
LUNA

Lucien offers to carry me back to the house but, despite him snapping the neck of his favorite security guard on my behalf, I can't allow him to.

I do not want to give in to the ache in my chest and the need to be close to him.

He hurt me. Not physically; he hurt me in a worse way than that. And I'm not just going to fall into his arms because he appeared from nowhere and played the hero.

After all, he only did it because he wants to keep me here. Right?

Walking beside me in the rain, Lucien's body is rigid, and his eyes focused ahead.

"I thought you liked him," I say, cradling my injured arm in front of me, trying to talk normally even though I'm shivering and I feel nauseous from the pain.

"Trent came to me as a pup. He has always been loyal. But I harbored no fondness for him." Lucien glances at me. "I made the rules very clear. I told him not to touch you."

"He unlocked my door. I'm not sure if he wanted to make it look like he'd found me escaping and brought me back, so you'd be pleased with him, or if he just wanted the thrill of the hunt."

Behind us, Lucien's dogs now pad along gently and calmly. Their snarls and barks are gone, and they seem more like pets than the vicious guard dogs that looked as if they would tear me to shreds if they caught hold of me.

Above, thunder booms and the rain intensifies. Lucien's hair is slick, water running down his face and tracing his chiseled features. He turns to me and folds his arms. "Would you please let me carry you back inside before you catch pneumonia?"

I look down at my bare feet. They are throbbing. Whatever I trod on earlier broke the skin and I know I'm still bleeding. My clothes are sodden, and I'm trembling. "All right. But not too fast. I already feel like I might throw up."

Lucien nods and gently lifts me into his arms. I wince as he accidentally brushes my injured shoulder, and he grimaces as though it hurt him too.

Inside, we do not go to my bedroom. Instead, he takes me to a door several feet down the hallway from the room I've been locked in for the past few days.

Lucien sets me down in front of the door and ushers me inside.

"Why aren't you taking me back to my own room?" I ask, lingering by the wall.

"Because your room is currently uninhabitable."

I raise my eyebrows at him.

"I lost my temper when I realized you were gone," he says, a little sheepishly.

As he moves, it's as if he's trying to do everything carefully and slowly so he doesn't startle me. This room is far more modern than the one I've been sleeping in.

The walls are a deep, matte black, broken only by large abstract art pieces in shades of grey and silver. The floor is polished concrete, cool beneath my bare feet, and a plush charcoal rug softens the space in front of an enormous bed.

The bed itself is a not the old fashioned four poster bed I've been using, but a low platform frame in dark wood, topped with sheets so black they seem to absorb light. The bedding looks sinfully soft, a mix of high thread count cotton and what appears to be silk.

Lucien strides over to the wall opposite the bed and presses a button on a small remote. A set of sleek black-out blinds raise up, casting interesting shadows across the room. When they are all the way up, a floor to ceiling window offers a panoramic view of the grounds, currently obscured by the night and the rain.

Lucien is standing by a minimalist desk of glass and chrome that sits in one corner. He is watching me carefully.

"This is your room," I say. It's not a question.

Lucien nods. "It is."

I try to fold my arms then remember how much my shoulder hurts.

"You're bleeding," he says as his tongue moistens his fangs. "I can taste it in the air."

"My foot." I gesture to my dirty feet. I'm still shivering.

"I'll run you a bath." He moves toward a large, frosted glass screen and I step sideways so I can see what's behind it. Of course, it's a sunken bathtub. Gloriously deep. He turns the taps and steam instantly fills the room. "Then I'll fix you up."

"Shouldn't we talk?" I sit on the edge of the bed, unable to keep standing for much longer.

"About?"

"The shadows." I tuck a strand of dripping wet hair behind my ear. "What they did when you rescued me."

Lucien's eyes flicker with those familiar red freckles. "You saw."

"Of course, I saw."

"You've seen them do that before? Move unnaturally? Do things they shouldn't?"

I bite my lower lip. "Maybe."

"We will talk," Lucien says dismissively. "But not now. First, we fix you."

He stands in front of me, then peels off his clothes. I try to look away but can't help the way my body reacts to the sight of him — naked, and damp, and beautiful.

Because that is the only word for it; beautiful.

When he drops his pants, I move closer and ask him to help me undress.

He unfastens my jeans, then stoops down as he eases them over my hips and helps me step out of them. My panties are next, and he pauses at the top of my thighs, his face tantalizingly close to my pussy.

Less than an hour ago, I hated him. I'd vowed never to talk to him again. To remember he's a liar, and a monster, and that he can't be trusted. But like this — close to him — I don't know how to resist him.

The memory of the way he spoke to me is fading. *This* seems like the real Lucien.

When Steven was nice to me, it was fake. It felt like a mask, a game, an act. I knew what lay beneath his smile. When my father treated me with kindness, it was because he felt guilty for hurting my mother or for shouting at me.

Their kindness was fake.

With Lucien, it seems the other way around; as if he's been trying to act like the big, tough vampire all this time when really he just wants to be loved.

I close my eyes and almost laugh at myself. For fuck's sake, Luna. Can you hear yourself?

When I open them, he is studying my sweater as if he's unsure how to remove it without hurting me. "Turn around," he says.

I obey him without hesitating, doing an excellent job of remembering that he is an evil monster who kidnapped me.

I feel his fingers on the hem of the sweater. They take hold of the fabric, then pull in opposite directions. Holy hell. He is *ripping* my sweater off me.

The sound of the fabric tearing makes me shudder and, slowly, my back is exposed. When the sweater is torn all the way from the hem to the neck, he eases it off my shoulders and over my arms.

Then he unfastens my bra and lets it fall to the floor.

Having him stand behind me, naked, his fingers on my skin, all I want to do is lean back against him and encourage him to cup my breasts with his large, strong hands.

I want to feel his thumbs on my nipples.

I want to lose myself in him and forget the way he looked at me in the pool, and the way Trent looked at me, and the sound his neck made when it snapped, and whatever the fuck happened to me when the shadows started to cocoon me as if I belonged to them.

Lucien moves away from me, and I hear him stepping into the bath. When I turn around, he's holding out his hand.

I take it and climb in, then he sits down and steadies me as I ease myself down into the water.

I don't resist him or ask him why he's sitting behind me; I just sink into him. I lean back and let him gently scoop water over my breasts and stomach.

A familiar scent fills the air. Blood. His blood. He has opened his wrist for me and is holding it to my lips. "It will heal you," he whispers. "Let me heal you."

I cradle his hand in mine, watching his blood drip into the bath and bloom like rose petals on the surface.

"I know you don't believe me, Luna, but all I want is your safety. It's all I've ever wanted."

"You're right," I answer him. "I don't believe you." But as he sighs and almost pulls away from me, I start to suck.

I seal my lips onto his wrist and suck his dark, deadly liquid into my mouth. With each drop that slides down my throat, the pain in my shoulder eases. The rest of the pain grows lighter too, quieter, softer.

My foot no longer hurts.

I am not exhausted.

But I *am* turned on.

I spin around and shift so I'm sitting in his lap, and our lips meet with a furious heat that makes me moan into his mouth. How have we missed each other so much when we have only been apart for a few hours?

"I'm sorry," he murmurs into my neck as he pushes my hair back over my shoulder. "I pushed you away. I was cruel. And I'm sorry." He sits back and meets my eyes.

And that is what makes him different. Because he apologized, and he means it.

I don't reply, just kiss him again and feel him begin to grow hard beneath me.

"Do you trust me?" he asks me the question for the second time.

His hands find my breasts and squeeze them lightly.

"Are you afraid of me?"

"I wasn't. From the second I arrived here, I felt safe with you. But after the pool. The way you looked at me..."

Lucien looks genuinely wounded. He draws in a deep breath, then eases me off him and leverages himself out of the bath. He strides away from me, back behind the screen, his bare ass looking so delicious I can barely pay attention to why he's leaving or what he's doing.

I follow, grabbing a towel, and find him standing at his desk. He is facing away from me, and when he turns around, he's holding something in his hand.

"Is that a stake?" I ask, frowning.

"A silver stake." He weighs the object up and down in his palm. It glints in the dim light. Outside, it is still raining, and the storm is still rumbling. He walks over to me and presses it into my hand, then he moves to the bed and lies down on his back, arms spread out at his sides. "There is some rope beneath the bed," he says.

Not quite understanding what he is doing, I reach under the bed and pull out a metal box. I lift the lid and look inside.

Two large pieces of rope. "They're made of..."

"Silver."

Lucien nods at me. "Give them to me."

I do as he says. They are heavy and take some effort to lift.

He takes the first, and his palm sizzles as it meets with the metal. My eyes widen, but Lucien simply holds on tighter and lays the silver rope across his extended arm. It hisses louder. His skin reddens and bubbles beneath it. He grits his teeth and groans.

"Now, you do the other."

"You want me to...?"

"I will be unable to move," he says. "Unless you free me."

As I realize what he's saying, and that I'm holding a stake in my hand, something begins to fizz deep in my core. I bite my lower lip, then crawl on top of him, metal rope in one hand, stake in the other.

He smirks as he looks up at me. "Fuck, you look beautiful up there, kitten." His eyes graze my breasts, and my stomach, and my face. Gently, I lay the rope over his other arm. He winces and his skin starts to burn.

"It's hurting you..."

"Rather me than you," he says. "I'll heal."

I press my empty palm to his chest. I can feel his heart beating beneath my hand. Faster than a human heart. "What now?"

"Now, I'm yours. You can do whatever you like." He glances at the stake I'm holding then meets my eyes, his gaze full of dark, quivering sin. "You choose how you end me, kitten. With the weapon in your hand... or the heat between your legs."

As he speaks, wetness spreads from my pussy to the tops of my thighs. I am soaked already, and he hasn't touched me yet.

"I can smell your arousal," he growls. "Did you know that?"

My cheeks start to flush. "You smell delicious." He strains against the rope and his skin burns harder. "You taste delicious, too. So, why don't you come here and sit on my face. Let me worship my queen."

I push my fingers through my hair then take off my glasses. Arousal and embarrassment hum on my skin. I am too big for that. I'll crush him, surely.

As if he can read my mind, he says, "There is nothing to be embarrassed about, Luna. I want to taste you. I want to feel you on top of me. Owning me. Taking the pleasure you deserve."

My entire body ignites under the heat of his words.

"Now, turn around and take a seat, kitten. Let me lick you into oblivion while you hold that stake above my heart."

Still holding the stake, gripping it hard, I do as he says; I turn around and ease back until my thighs are either side of his face. I hover above him, but he growls, "Sit," and so I thrust down hard onto his lips.

As he seals his tongue over my clit, he groans loudly and mumbles something I can't hear because I'm groaning, too.

My pleasure builds and I lean forward, holding the tip of the stake above his heart. I have never felt so powerful. He's right; I could end him. Right now, I could drive his stake into his heart, and he would disintegrate beneath me.

He has given me more than an apology; he has given me the ultimate control over his body.

As moonlight shines through the window, illuminating us in an otherworldly glow, Lucien lavishes my pussy with his lips and tongue. Heat explodes like fireworks throughout my body as a white-hot ache builds between my legs. I moan and clench my thighs around his head as he increases the intensity of his attention, every flick of his skilled tongue sending me spiraling closer to the edge.

I drop the stake and arch forward, taking him deep into my mouth as he groans up into my pussy.

I suck hard, making him buck his hips into my mouth, and the sound of his pleasure merges with the sound of his pain as his skin strains against his restraints.

"Lucien," I moan around his cock. "I'm so close. Oh fuck, I'm so close."

His taste floods my tongue as I suck him even harder, and he groans louder. "That's it, kitten. Drain me. Take it all."

As I feel him stiffen, his cock twitching in my mouth, I pull away, drop the stake, and rip the ropes away from his hands, desperate for him to hold me.

I look down at his wrists. They are red raw and blistered. "You're hurt," I whisper.

"There's blood in the drawer." He gestures to the bedside table, but when I open it, there is nothing there.

I try the other. Nothing there either.

"I'll be okay." He reaches for me. "Come here and let me make you purr, kitten. You were so close."

"Not while you're hurt." I shake my head. Then I meet his eyes. "Use me."

Lucien's gaze darkens in an instant. "No."

I straddle him, his cock already hard again, pressing against my ass. "Use me," I say, scooping my hair back from my neck to expose what I'm certain is a delicious looking vein.

What am I doing? Why do I want to feel him pierce my skin so badly? Why does the idea of my blood in his mouth make pleasure skitter down my spine?

I lean over him, and slide onto his cock at the same time, holding my neck above his lips.

"Bite me, Lucien. Drink me."

A low, animalistic growl escapes his lips. He grabs hold of me, rough, large hands holding me still. And then there it is... the pain and the release. His fangs puncture my skin and as he sucks, and sucks, I thrust down onto him, slipping a hand between us so I can touch my aching clit.

My eyes flutter.

He is still drinking. I pull back a little, but he holds me tight.

My heart begins to pound wildly against my ribcage as panic sets in. What have I done?

Lucien stops abruptly and practically throws me off of him, jumping to his feet.

His lips and chin are stained with my blood. His eyes are dark, and his fangs are visible. He lunges at me, and before I can blink, he has me pinned against the wall, his forearms on either side of my head, his hips grinding into mine. "You taste so fucking good, Luna." He spins me around, licks a fast, furious line down my spine with the tip of his tongue, then drops to his knees.

"I don't know what I want more... your blood or your cunt."

Hearing that word on his lips makes me groan and jut my ass out toward him. Lucien holds onto my hips.

"Not your tongue. Your cock." I reach for him and drag him to his feet. "Fuck me." I look over my shoulder. "But fuck me like a vampire. Fuck me like you aren't afraid of hurting me."

His eyes flash. Pleasure rolls across his features and his breath hitches in his chest. "That's what you want?"

"That's what I want."

"Then you feed from me at the same time," he says. "So I *know* I won't hurt you."

He wraps a large, muscular arm around my chest, pressing it against my throat. Then he opens his wrist and presses it to my lips. At the same time, he slams into me so hard I think I'm going to go straight through the wall.

My eyes flutter closed. I cry out and his blood trickles down my chin onto my breasts. He uses it to moisten my nipples. His other hand is between my legs, and his cock is pounding into me from behind.

It is all happening so hard and so fast that I can hardly breathe.

Every thought disappears from my head. My vision blurs. The room becomes dark, and the darkness cocoons us both.

We are caught in a dark whirlwind of lust, and I cannot see any way to escape it. Not now. Not tomorrow. Not ever.

Lucien has me, and I have him.

This is how it was meant to be.

Us.

Like this.

Forever.

CHAPTER 31
LUNA

When I climax, I scream so loudly I feel like the window might splinter into a million tiny pieces. Lucien comes again, too. Hard. Fast. Hot.

He holds me against him as his thrusts slow. His hands move up my body. He cradles me tightly. Everything feels too sensitive, too alert, too turned on.

His thumbs brush my nipples and I whimper.

He plays with me for a while, testing which pieces of me are still tender. What will make me gasp and what will make me lean into him.

"Have you ever fucked a human before?" The question leaves my lips before I have chance to stop it.

"Not like that," he whispers, breath warm on my neck.

"Have you ever loved a human before?" I stiffen a little, waiting for his answer.

Finally, he says, "No."

"Do you love me?" I turn in his arms and meet his gaze. He

tries to look away, but I cup his face in my hand and make him look at me. "You killed for me. You've protected me. Why?"

His jaw twitches. His words echo in my head. *Stay out of my business.*

"Lucien... why am I here?"

"Yes," he says, taking hold of my arms. "Yes, I do love you, Luna."

I stare up at him. I want to tell him I love him, too. But there is something I need first.

I need the truth.

"Then tell me why I'm here."

Lucien hesitates, then strides away from me, bracing his hands behind his head, elbows jutting out to the side. "Because it is my duty to protect you."

"Why?"

"Because you are special."

"And you love me?"

"Yes."

"Then tell me the truth, Lucien."

There is a long pause.

"I can't."

"If you loved me, you'd tell me."

"I cannot tell you. Not yet. It is for your own safety. And I don't truly understand it yet myself. So, you'll just have to trust me."

Fury blooms in my chest. Trust him? How can I? After everything, he still won't tell me what's really going on.

"You think because of that little game back there, I'll trust you now?" I stride over to the bed and lift up one of the chains. "You think I don't know you could have ripped out of these if you wanted to? You expect me to believe you gave me that kind of power when you won't give me a simple answer? You're playing with me, Lucien. I'm nothing but a toy to you. A toy. You're manipulating me just like—"

"Don't you *dare* compare me to him." Lucien closes the gap between us in an instant. "I told you I love you. Do you know what that means? I haven't said those words for nearly five hundred years, Luna."

"He told me that, too. Steven. He told me he loved me."

"*I* mean it."

My hands are shaking. I tilt my chin and meet his eyes. "I don't believe you, Lucien. I think I am still an object to you. A thing you want to possess. Like every other man in my life. You want to own me."

Fury rages in his eyes. He gets up from the bed and storms over to the large flat mirror above the desk. In one movement, he rips it from the wall, smashes it over his knee, and grabs a shard of glass.

I press myself against the wall, shaking, convinced he's going to come for me. But instead, he presses the tip of the shard to his chest. Right in the center.

"What are you doing?" My eyes widen.

He presses harder, and harder, plunging the glass deeper and deeper. Blood drips down his chest, his abs, over his bellybutton, his hips, his cock. More and more as the glass digs in deeper and deeper. He drags it down, his fist curled around it, blood dripping from his palm too.

I cannot move. I am transfixed.

Finally, he drops the shard of glass to the floor. It lands with a thud on the polished concrete. He is breathing heavily. His skin is already trying to heal itself, but instead of letting it, he thrusts his fingers into the wound and, with a roar that shakes the entire room, splits his chest open. Completely. Open.

I scream and slam my hands over my mouth. "Lucien, stop!"

He picks up the piece of glass and drops to his knees in front of me. With blood dripping down to coat his body and the floor, he lifts the blade and holds it above his ribs.

I can see his heart beating. Muscle, and sinew, and skin, and blood.

I can *hear* his heart beating.

I can smell the blood.

He looks down, glass tight in his hand, and presses it to the rib directly above his dark, quivering heart. His hand moves slowly. He releases a loud roar, holding his chest open with one hand while the other makes small, considered movements above his ribs.

Finally, he stops. He raises his gaze and catches mine. He throws the glass to the floor and points to his chest. His skin is starting to heal, to slowly creep back in toward itself.

But I see now what he has done.

He has carved something into his ribs.

My name.

LUNA.

He lurches for me, grabs my hand, and presses my fingertips to the letters. I trace them slowly, transfixed by the rhythm of his heart and the feel of my name. When I look up at him, he takes my chin in his hand and growls, "Now, do you believe me, Luna? Do you believe that I love you? Or must I rip out my heart and throw it at your feet?"

My hand is still in his chest. His muscles and his skin are sewing themselves back together. If I don't move, I'll be trapped inside him. Literally. *Inside* him. I tug my hand, try to move it, but he holds it still.

"Do you believe me?" He breathes.

I don't reply. Instead, shaking, I lower my lips to his exposed ribs and kiss the place where he carved my name. When I glance up at him through hooded eyes, with bloodied lips, I whisper, "I believe you, Lucien."

He frees my hand, scoops me into his arms, and throws me back onto the bed. His eyes flash. "Did I hurt you?"

"No."

"Can I fuck you again?"

"Yes."

His lips find mine, and he holds me tight against him.

"But after... you're going to tell me everything." I meet his eyes. Not a question. A statement. "If you love me, you'll tell me everything."

He trails his thumb along my lower lip. He is panting, the gaping wound in his chest almost healed now. "I'll tell you everything. I promise."

CHAPTER 32
NIX

The mansion looks just as it always did, but it has been centuries since I called this place home. Its imposing silhouette cuts a dark shape against the night sky, a behemoth of stone and history looming over meticulously manicured lawns.

I stand in the shadows beneath the silver birch trees. Cerberus pants loudly, his breath blooming hot pale clouds into the night air.

The grand oak doors, ornately carved with our family crest, remain firmly shut. How many times had I walked through those doors, side by side with Lucien, blood-drunk and laughing after a successful hunt? Now, they stand as a barrier, keeping me out of the life my brother has built for himself.

The life he chose to exclude me from.

As if sensing my thoughts, Cerberus lets out a low growl. I place a calming hand on his head.

"Patience, old friend," I murmur. "Our time will come."

My eyes are drawn to a warm glow emanating from an

upstairs window. There they are - Lucien and the human girl, Luna. Even from this distance, I can see the tenderness in my brother's embrace, the way he holds her as if she's something precious and fragile.

A smirk tugs at my lips. "Well, well," I mutter to Cerberus. "It seems my brother has gone and given his heart to a human. How... quaint. But does he know what she is? That's the question."

The dog huffs, as if sharing my disdain for my brother's weakness.

I watch as Luna leans into Lucien's embrace, her face turned up to his. The intimacy of the moment is almost palpable. It would be touching if it weren't so pathetic.

Lucien seems entirely focused on the girl; his usually sharp senses dulled by... what? Love? Lust? Whatever it is, it's made him careless. He doesn't sense my presence, doesn't feel the weight of my gaze. How the mighty have fallen.

"Oh, Lucien," I sigh, shaking my head. "You always were a romantic fool. Don't you see? Love is a liability. Power is the only currency that matters. I thought you'd learned that long ago."

As if he can hear me, Lucien stiffens suddenly, glancing toward the window. I melt further into the shadows, though I know he can't possibly detect my presence. Not yet anyway.

I've come too far, planned too carefully, to reveal myself now. But soon... oh, very soon, my dear brother will know exactly what I have in store for him and his precious human.

"Come, Cerberus," I say, turning away from the mansion. "We have work to do."

As we walk away, blending into the night, I can't help but smile. Lucien thinks he's protecting the girl, but he has no idea of the forces he's up against. Of the power that's within my grasp.

"Don't worry, brother," I whisper to the night. "Soon you'll see that my way is the only way. And when you do…" I pause, savoring the thought. "Well, let's just say the Thornfield brothers will rule this world together. Whether you like it or not."

Cerberus growls in agreement, his massive form a shadow at my side. My plans falling into place like pieces on a chessboard. It's only a matter of time before I have them both exactly where I want them.

And when I do, the real game begins.

The Covenant of Shadows will be awakened, and with it, a new era for our kind.

∼

Thank you for reading **Luna**
(Covenant of Shadows, Book One)
I'm sorry to leave you on a cliffhanger,
but Book Two is available for preorder now!
You can grab it here.

In the meantime, if you'd love to read the a free spicy scene, plus stay up to date with special print editions and audiobooks, sign up for my newsletter.

And, as always, if you enjoyed reading Luna, please consider leaving a review on Amazon, Goodreads, or TikTok.

You can also keep reading for a sneek peak from 'Nova' (Book One, The Phoenix Prophecy.

'Nova' is a complete nine book series.
A super spicy whychoose set in the same universe as 'Luna'.

LOVE LUNA?

If you enjoyed Luna, I would be incredibly grateful if you'd leave a review so that others can discover it too!

As an independent author, reviews are one of the most important tools we have to help spread the word about our books.

Even if it's short, it will be *hugely* appreciated.

You can leave reviews on Amazon, Goodreads, or Storygraph - just search for Luna by Cara Clare and hit 'leave a review'.

About Cara

If you love why-choose romance, magic, super-hot mages, and even hotter RH scenes, then we're destined to be friends.

I mean it when I say I love keeping in touch with my readers. Come say hi over on TikTok or Instagram or join my newsletter.

I have a direct store on my website, where you can shop for merch, signed copies, and sign up for my newsletter:

www.caraclare.com

- amazon.com/Cara-Clare/e/B09ZQRV4QG
- tiktok.com/@caraclareauthor
- instagram.com/caraclareauthor

CHAPTER ONE

NOVA

It is almost sunset. The air vibrates with heat. Sticky on my skin and in my mouth. On stage, the head of the Ridgemore Anti Magick Alliance is spouting his usual vitriol into a handheld microphone. He holds it too close to his mouth. It screeches when he raises his voice. He's almost reached the climax of his speech.

"Together, we will put those filthy fucking supers back in the shadows where they belong!"

The crowd roars. The noise is like a swarm of insects buzzing in my ears. My heart hammers harder in my chest.

"Here in Ridgemore, we know what needs to be done. And we're not afraid to do it!"

Another roar.

Johnny slurps warm beer from an almost-empty can, wipes his mouth with his arm, and growls in agreement. His left fist is clenched. Cracked skin stretches over his white knuckles.

He drops the can to the ground, grinds it into the earth with his foot, then takes hold of my wrist. "We're leaving."

"We're not staying for the music?" I ask, trailing after him as he strides through the crowd.

He doesn't bother to respond.

In the truck, he turns to stare at me. His lips curl into a smile. He almost looks handsome, although it's been a long time since he was anything but monstrous in my eyes.

He leans over and drags a finger down my throat toward my chest. I'm wearing my copper hair long and loose. He flicks it out of the way and his eyes darken. "Did it feel good?"

I swallow hard.

"Did it feel good? Wearing our mark tonight?"

I bite the inside of my cheek so I don't flinch when he touches my red, raw skin. The emblem he burned into me a week ago. The symbol of the Anti Magick Alliance. Right there on my chest, above my heart, for everyone to see. Another scar to add to my collection.

"Of course, baby." I fix my eyes on him, saying what he wants to hear.

"Shame we couldn't show them the other one." His gaze lurches from my chest to my legs. Thankfully, the brand on my thigh healed a long time ago, so when he reaches it, pinching me through my jeans, I'm able to smile.

His fingers tug at my waistband. "Take them off."

"Shouldn't we wait until we get home?" I've perfected this tone; sultry, unthreatening, polite.

"I don't think I can. Not now that you've got me all riled up." His tongue darts out to moisten his lower lip.

I glance at the clock on the dash. "You wanted to see that show. On TV. It starts soon."

He stops. His body has stiffened. "Right." He sits back, takes hold of the wheel, grits his teeth. "After, then."

I reach over and squeeze his knee. "After."

~

By the time we get back, the apartment is dark. Johnny doesn't turn on the lights, just heads straight for the couch and grabs the remote.

"I'll be right there. I'm just going to the bathroom." I'm lingering in the kitchen. The bathroom door is open. I'm half expecting him to tell me I should wait, but he simply grunts, opens a can, and lights a cigarette.

Closing the door behind me, I lean against it and flick on the light. It takes me a moment to adjust, then I step forward and examine myself in the mirror. I look like I haven't eaten properly in weeks. Not because I'm gaunt or skinny—I've never been gaunt or skinny in my entire life—but because everything about me has lost its shine.

My hair is flat. Once a vivid shade of auburn, it's now closer to rust than fire. Instead of sparkling, my eyes—my most distinguishing feature; one blue, one brown—are dark. Like murky water from the bottom of the ocean. Even my skin is muted.

I press my palm against my cheek and sigh. I'm turning into a monochrome version of myself, and I don't know how to stop it.

It probably has something to do with the fact that I haven't eaten or slept properly in months. Since Johnny got tied up with the Anti Magick Alliance—the 'A.M.A', as they call themselves—his behavior has become increasingly erratic.

He lives on cigarettes, beer, and whatever he can steal from the bar he works at. He rarely thinks to bring food home for me, and as my wages go straight into our joint bank account—an account I have no access to—I'm left scrounging off my colleagues at the pharmacy or, sometimes stealing from the grocery store.

The most vivid thing about me now is the mark on my chest. The series of interconnecting triangles, scorched into me, with a blood-red tear drop tattooed in their center.

I trace my fingertips over the bumpy, raised flesh. I can still hear myself screaming.

When he tattooed my thigh, inked me with his initials, the pain was no worse than the kind I'd experienced a million times before.

But the poker... that was a new level of torture.

"Nova?" Johnny's voice bleeds through the bathroom door. "Nova, get in here. It's starting."

I inhale sharply. Hold my breath for longer than usual, grip the edge of the basin, then walk back to the living room.

He's still on the couch, staring at the TV. He looks sideways at me and curls his finger to beckon me over. When I'm in front of him, he tears his eyes away from the screen and puts down his can. He tugs at my shirt.

"Lean forward." He tugs it again. "Show me."

Closing my eyes, I pull back my hair and lean over him.

I hear him suck in his breath. "Fuck. Tor did a good job." He looks up at me, eyes twinkling. "Good birthday present, huh?"

Oh, yeah, I feel like saying. *Best birthday present I've ever had—being tied down while you and your buddy melt my skin with a red-hot poker. Being left with this disgusting, fascist symbol etched below my throat for the rest of my life.*

"All the guys are doing it now." Johnny's still staring at the scar, but his hands are creeping up beneath my shirt. "Getting their wives and girlfriends marked." He pulls me closer and grazes my stomach with his teeth. Now he's chewing on me. Like a dog slobbering on a bone.

He pulls me into his lap and licks from my throat to my chest. As his tongue laps my scarred flesh, my stomach twists. His cock is rock hard. He groans into my neck, then he flips me over, down onto the couch, on my back, beneath him.

His hands are everywhere. But I'm somewhere else.

I turn and look at the TV. The show he was so desperate to watch has started.

"Johnny..." His weight is pressing down on me. I try to move my arm, but it's trapped between his torso and mine.

He's grunting now. Thrusting, even though he's not inside me yet.

I keep my eyes fixed on the screen. Johnny has never been into Friday-night talk shows but, this week, a member of the A.M.A. is being interviewed alongside Nico Varlac. America's biggest supernatural celebrity. A werewolf and a self-appointed do-gooder with a mission to unite supers and humans.

Nico is waving at the studio audience. His hair is jet black. His shoulders ripple as he moves across to take his seat on the guest couch. I sometimes think Sam would have looked like Nico. If he hadn't...

"What the hell?" Johnny stops moving.

I turn my head. His eyes lock onto mine. He pinches my face between his thumb and his index finger, and squeezes. Hard. "What the hell are you looking at?" He growls. "Are you looking at him?" He jerks my face toward the TV. "While I'm fucking you, you're thinking about a filthy mage super?"

I open my mouth to speak, but he moves his hand to my throat and stands, pulling me with him. He holds me there for a moment, then throws me to the floor.

"Are you a sympathizer?" He steps toward me.

I bring my knees up to my chest and scoot backward. There is no point in answering him.

His shadow falls over me. Illuminated by the glare of the TV, his face is cast in a light bluish hue. He's skinny, but cruel enough for it not to matter. He lunges for me. As he moves, something happens.

The air shifts. A rushing sound fills my ears, as if I'm on a train and hurtling through a tunnel. I slam my eyes closed.

When I open them, Johnny is still moving, but it's like he's wading through treacle. Like time has slowed to a fraction of its normal speed. I stagger to my feet and duck sideways just as everything roars back to life.

Johnny stumbles and falls into the TV. It shunts backward on the stand but stays upright. He turns around. He's flexing his fingers at his sides, then his right hand moves, quick as a flash, to his belt. He pulls out his pocketknife.

I take a step backward, scanning the room for something—anything—I can use to keep him at bay. I look past him to the bathroom, but there's no way I'll make it in time.

He stares me down. For a moment, neither of us moves. I'm barely even breathing. Then he comes for me.

I jump sideways and race around the back of the couch. He trips on the corner of the rug. He's drunk and clumsy. Probably the only thing in my favor right now.

He rights himself. I know I need to stop him. Fear pulses through my limbs. I'm in the corner of the room. I have nowhere to go. The only thing I can reach is the vanilla-scented candle his mother bought us last Christmas. The only ornamental thing in the entire apartment. I grab it and hurl it across the room.

I'm aiming for his body. Anywhere on his body. But I've misjudged, and it's going to hit the floor instead.

As it does, a jolt of electricity shoots through me. So violent that I'm flung back against the wall. The candle hits the ground, and then...

Flames.

Huge, billowing flames come from nowhere. They spread sideways, casting a shield of fire between Johnny and me.

He's on the other side of them. He stops, knife still in his hand. "What the...?"

The fire is spreading, snaking across the floor toward my feet. But I'm not afraid. It licks my bare toes. I know it should feel hot.

It doesn't.

Johnny yells and drops his knife. He levers himself over the back of the couch, heading for the door. Before he can reach it, a wall of flames appears in front of him. He turns. More flames. He turns again.

He's surrounded.

I watch him panicking. His eyes wide, he starts to cough. Smoke is curling around the flames, enveloping his legs, his arms, his chest.

I step forward. The heat tickles my skin. As I move, the fire moves too.

Johnny is staring at me through the fire. His dark eyes lock with mine. I tilt my head and take him in.

He's the only boy I've ever been with. The boy who took me away from my last and shittiest foster home when I was fifteen. When I was lost, and he seemed like the sun and the moon. The boy who later taught me to fear him, to obey him. The boy who told me magick was evil, and that supers weren't to be trusted.

As my thoughts spiral, I tilt back my head. My chest is tight. I open my mouth and scream. The sound reverberates through my bones as it leaves my body. The flames burn higher and harder, and I swear it's like the louder I scream, the bigger they get.

SNEAK PEEK

When I stop screaming, Johnny is staring at me. "Witch! You're a fucking witch!" He points at me. He's afraid. I look at his pants. He's pissed himself.

A tower of ferocious heat shimmers between us.

His expression changes. He puts his palms up, eyes wide. Like a mouse being hunted by a hawk. He's shaking his head now, trying to surrender. Trying to buy himself some time. "Nova. Baby. Please."

I turn away.

I feel the force of the heat on my back.

"Goodbye, Johnny."

∼

The entire Phoenix Prophecy series is available now and is free to read in Kindle Unlimited.

You can grab it here.

ACKNOWLEDGMENTS

'Luna' marks the start of a new chapter in my life (excuse the pun!). A lot of things have happened in the past year, during which I've been planning and writing Luna's story, and I have to thank those who have supported me through it.

There aren't really enough words, or at least enough *adequate* words, to express how much I appreciate the people who have helped me laugh, cry, and be joyful in one of the most difficult but incredibly empowering periods of my life.

So, in no particular order... the biggest of thankyous to:

My sister Maya Tate, who really is the big sister even though she's the little sister.

Sacha Black, the soul friend who found me and refused point blank to let me go.

The Beswicks, who are the most wonderful, gorgeous, beautiful humans I've ever met.

The Cambridge Author crew, who are just an incredible bunch of people to know.

The Ladies of The Apocalypse, who are and always have been the ones who get it.

The many terrible, hillarious and good-for-now-but-not-f0r-life Bumble and Hinge dates who have provided hours of entertainment for everyone mentioned above. And kept my therapist in business.

And, of course, my readers. You changed my life. You gave me the confidence to step into the version of myself I always wanted to be, and I will never stop being grateful to you.

Printed in Great Britain
by Amazon

46565127R00129